The Guilty

of

The Korean War

by

Jerry Carson

To Jim
From Marino
[signature]
Jerry

Copyright 2002
by
Jerry Carson

Cover design by Renny James

ISBN 0-9713832-9-4

Word Wright International
P.O. Box 1785
Georgetown, TX 78627
http://www.WordWright.biz

Printed in the United States of America

Dedicated to

Jack, Hal, Matt, and all who went and came back.
Some returned whole;
some not whole;
all with new baggage.

Bill and all who went but did not come back.

"Bert" and all who spent their time in the hell
of a POW camp;
suffered under an Army SYA;
and now share the anonymity
of presidential amnesty.

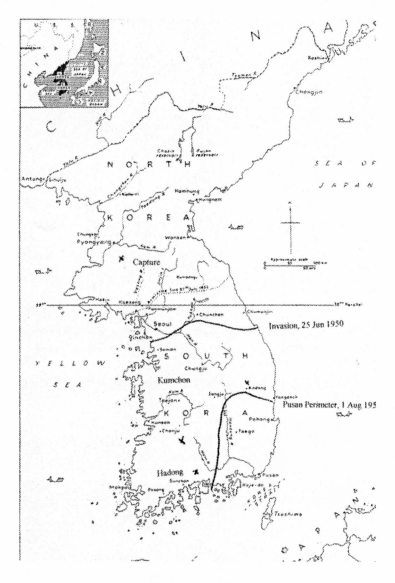

Korea – 1950
Office of the Chief of Military History
Department of the Army
Center of Military History
Washington, D.C., 1982
Army Map Service, Corps of Engineers

Chapter 1

In the Beginning

His senses unconsciously pulled his awareness from the drone of the courtroom to the memory of sounds and scenes from long past. When officially notified of the charge against him, the memories and nightmares had returned. Sounds and scenes from that unhappy past demanded attention.

"Tanks! Gawd! They's tanks!"

The startled young second lieutenant swiveled his head and squinted north along the road, shading his eyes against the South Korean sun. Low, just above the highlands along the Han River to the west, the sun cast a deceptive crystal sheen over the slime of the flooded rice paddies on each side of the valley road.

"There. At the base of that far hill, Sir." The corporal pointed.

For a fleeting second the officer imagined the tank's noise as they clanked into view some 5,000 yards in the distance.

"Well," the lieutenant sighed. "At least regiment was right about one thing. It's a North Korean tank column, and we're supposed to stop them."

"But, Sir," the young corporal almost controlled the quiver in his voice. "I unloaded the ammo. We ain't got bazookas, recoilless, mortars, nothing but them .30 caliber machine guns."

After a silent moment the lieutenant looked back from the apparition of death clinking toward the small road junction his pick-up platoon had been ordered to hold.

"Yes, I know." He smiled thinly at Corporal Bert Cronwette. "Get your squad dug in and buttoned down. If they have infantry..."

Second Lieutenant Hunley turned without finishing the

warning and ran toward the pathetic roadblock his provisional platoon was to man against a North Korean Peoples Army tank column.

❈   ❈   ❈

"I see the Andong Junction, Comrade Observer."

Over the noise inside the Russian-made T-34 tank ripe with the acrid fumes from the diesel fuel, the Russian Officer Observer mumbled an acknowledgement and eased up into the open turret hatch. He adjusted his binoculars, carefully studied the distant small cluster of huts, and eased back into the tank.

"Yes, Comrade, you are right. An enemy road block waits for us."

"Me goul?"

"Yes," the Russian Officer smiled, "an American road block."

"Oh, my. We must do as the vaunted General MacArthur says. We must turn and run at the sight of Americans."

The Russian's head jerked toward the North Korean. Then he saw the crinkle of skin around the tank commander's eyes. The Russian Officer smiled too at the absurd bluster of the American General. These hardened veterans of the defeat of the Nationalist Chinese Army were a fine fighting force. They had run from no enemy.

"We have no time for them, my friend. We are due east of Osan before 24 hundred hours and cannot pause for this pitiful military insult." The Russian Officer patted the Tank Commander's shoulder and added. "We go through this junction. We do not stop."

"Comrade gunner," the tank commander smiled, "When in range, we fire as we roll."

The road the tank column followed led generally from east to west. A curve around the hills turned the road temporarily to the south as it approached the junction at Andong. Just south of Andong the road would return to its principal direction of Chungju.

Lieutenant Hunley paused at the radio hut. He started to ask but when he looked in the operator shook his head. "These batteries just ain't strong enough to carry over them Korean hills to batallion, Sir."

"Keep trying." The Lieutenant turned and continued his way to the junction.

"All set, Sergeant?" the Lieutenant asked.

"All ready, Sir. What fun we could have with just one good mortar and a few rounds of armor-piercing." Sergeant Reuben J. Heintzman shook his head.

"It'll be one-sided," the lieutenant offered. "We have our orders."

"I'll get 'em buttoned up, Sir."

"Hold fire 'till we see infantry. No reason to waste what we have on tanks." Lieutenant Hunley started to his left as Sgt. Heintzman turned to his right. The thin line at the road block was six Browning Automatic Rifles (BAR), one heavy, water-cooled .30 caliber, one light, air-cooled .30 caliber machine gun, and six M-1s. All held in nervous and sweating hands by worried GIs who, to the man in his young life, had never heard a round fired in anger.

Both the Officer and the NCO returned to the middle of the thin line in the gathering dusk.

"Sergeant, I left a duffel at regiment with clothes I haven't worn since leaving Ft. Benning. When assigned to this Provisional Unit, they told me you were a veteran and my ass would be safe if I listened to you."

The lieutenant looked straight at the older soldier. "I'm listening."

"Thanks, but no help, Sir." The Sergeant shook his head. "Five years ago if I saw a Kraut column like that coming toward my road block, I'd have a couple of heavy mortars back where Cronwette is with the reserve squad. Cases of high explosive anti-tank ready. A 155 would anchor each of the two sides of the road."

A grim silence followed for what seemed like long minutes.

3

"They didn't give us what we need, did they?" The lieutenant calmly broke the silence.

"Can't really blame regiment, Sir. What we need right here, right now, is not to be found in the whole damn Far East Command. When I first arrived in Tokyo, I was casual for a couple of weeks and temporarily assigned ordnance. We spent most of our time trying to recover worn-out machine gun barrels, and cleaning crud off .30 caliber rounds for serviceability." Sergeant Heintzman shook his head as he finished.

"Surely the army has heavy stuff left over from World War II. That was only five years ago, Sergeant."

"The big brass in the Pentagon, Sir, are convinced the Russians will attack Germany. That area has received all serviceable and heavy equipment in preparation for the Russians. We have the little stuff scrounged from the islands here in the Pacific." The Sergeant reported.

The young lieutenant sighed audibly. "Well, Sergeant, the curtain will go up, soon." The lieutenant raised one shoulder in disgust, "For whatever good this crossroad is to the North Koreans."

"Oh, they mean to take it, Sir. Regimental G-3 said the lead elements of the 25th Division had a big fight with the North Koreans east of here. Almost a stand-off. The North Koreans are believed to have side-stepped and are trying to drive through here to Yechon, to our west. The road there allows them to turn north to Chungju. Eighth Army wants to make a stand at Chungju. A drive by those tanks," Sergeant Heintzman pointed to the approaching specter of doom, "puts the NKPA behind Chungju."

"A simple envelopment in force," the lieutenant observed tiredly.

"Yes, Sir, and us little boys with sling shots are here to stop a tank column." Sergeant Heintzman sighed.

After a moment of obvious sad thoughts, the young officer turned and headed for the rear of the village. He didn't bother to stop at the radio hut.

Corporal Cronwette reported. "Sir."

"The tanks are almost close enough to start firing. Get your men buttoned up. Tell them to hang tight. Only if the column includes infantry do we fire. Got it?"

With no further words the young officer turned back toward the junction. Corporal Cronwette turned to his squad.

"Okay. Listen up, men." Bert talked as he went from hole to hole along the squad's line while the men continued working at their foxholes. "Stay down low. Don't leave the hole 'n don't waste ammo on no tanks. Look for infantry. Don't..."

The words were lost in the monstrous tearing sound of the first incoming round as it passed over the village and exploded in a rice paddy behind them. A geyser of slime blossomed into the gathering dusk.

"In the hole!" Bert dove into his own foxhole as he yelled.

The second round shook the South Korean earth in front of the junction.

Sergeant Heintzman jumped into one of the gun pits at the road. He could have easily pictured the routine artillery procedure of one over, one short, and on target. He knew with the tank's forward movement, no adjustment would be needed for the tanker's next round. It was on target at the junction.

The world erupted in earth-trembling explosions around Bert. Without thought he flung both arms out to steady the sides of his rotten stinking hole in South Korea's fetid paddy region. His foxhole-buddy stared at him wide-eyed as he too huddled into the other side of the cramped hole. Shaking knees brushed each other.

All of the South Korea in which the frightened green GIs had a life's interest now trembled and shook. A hot July day in 1950 threatened to be their last.

The tanks rumbled to the junction. As they approached, the lead tank concentrated fire on the center of the gun emplacements while the second tank fired on those at the left end of the line and the third attacked the opposite end.

As it rolled inexorably past the junction, the lead tank traversed its turret and began a seemingly laconic destruction of the huts of the village. By systematic fire and movement the tanks transfigured the South Korean village of Andong from crossroad home for humble peasants to rubble.

5

As each of the tanks entered the devastation left by the preceding behemoth its smoking muzzle searched for any viable target or large pile of debris. The lead tank passed the last hut. The turret traversed to the now fire-lit fresh dirt of the reserve squad's foxholes. Bert trembling, shrank as deep as he could into his hole.

"Shoulda dug deeper." He moaned from behind gritted teeth.

The blast of the shell's detonation seemed inside Bert's helmet. He cringed. The world of his senses instantly shrank to the bottom of his hole. He heard the tank rumble past.

Bert inched to the top of the foxhole and peeped over the rim. An eerie light from the many fires lit by the shelling illuminated the area at the rear of the once-living village. A black cloud of dust, smoke, and small bits of debris darkened the scene further. The cloud hovered over the destruction, as if to cloak the slaughter.

"Tank!" Bert flung himself back into his life-hole.

The explosion must have been just at the rim. His eyes stung. His ears rang. His shoulders tensed voluntarily. Dirt rained down inside the back of his fatigue jacket. He spit dirt mixed with blood from a tooth-lacerated cheek lining. He didn't hear but rather felt the movement of his foxhole buddy. He looked in time to see Caparelli scratch frantically to the top of the foxhole.

"No!" Bert screamed as he lunged to pull Caparelli back.

What fell into Bert's lap was not his buddy but a horribly mangled mess of blood, torn flesh, and riddled fatigues.

As the panicked GI had struggled to flee the inexorable shelling, one of the tank's machine guns had nearly bisected the body. Now all the horrors of death sank into Bert's lap in the bottom of the stinking hole. Bert stiffened back the few remaining inches to the side of the hole. Spasmodically, as if controlled by some exterior mechanism, his elbows raked the dirt in a bizarre and useless effort to propel himself from the horror that had invaded his life.

He didn't realize his mouth had opened wide in the autonomic scream of pure terror. What had been a living, joking, and happy buddy was now garbage. Time became a lost commodity. He neither knew, saw, nor heard anything as he cringed in his hole. How long? Was he also dead?

It was quiet. Was that death?

The clanking of the tanks and the jaw-rattling explosions of the shells had stopped. He shook his head lightly. His ears detected no sound other than the roar from the recent explosions. He eased toward the lip of the foxhole.

Bert struggled to get his traumatized body to respond to his wants. Shaking, he pulled himself out of the hole. Once over the rim he could see an inferno, the only noise the crackle and rush of air around the burning debris that was now Andong. A surrealistic panorama spread before him. No cluster of peasant huts remained. They had been replaced by a pile of burning, smoking, and scrambled rubble.

Momentarily awed by the destruction, he shook his head and turned his attention to his former line of foxholes. A series of gaping shell holes had taken their places. In a daze, Bert moved along the holes as though he struggled through a sea of molasses. Slowly, small and large muscles in his cramped legs began to do his bidding. The eerie crackling of the fires and moaning of the wind from the inferno sang a dirge to shroud the disaster.

Empty pits torn rudely from the earth answered his visual search. In only one hole did he find life. Private Onterro had sustained a head laceration and Bert began tending to the wound with sulfa and a first aid-pack bandage.

A call from the darkness startled Bert. "Corporal?"

Bert automatically hunkered down in the hole beside Onterro as he scanned to the call's location. A wet, dripping, and slimy mess struggled from the ripeness of the rice paddy.

"Johnston?" Bert squinted to be sure of the identity.

"I hid, Corporal, hid out." The frightened GI's voice shook as he shambled forward.

Bert looked at the slime that glistened awkwardly from the wet GI reflecting the world of fire around him. Bert's memory focused crazily on a Japanese dancer he had watched in a Japanese burlesque attempting a strip-tease, her sequin-dappled breasts reflecting sparkles of light.

He shook his head to clear the imagery.

"I reckon we all did our best to hide...someplace. C'mon and help Ontero here. I have to get up there and report. When you get him patched up good, look around for useable arms an' ammo. We're behind enemy lines now." Bert started away then turned back to Johnston. "Uh, and stay down-wind of us, okay?"

All Bert saw at the junction was more of where the provisional platoon had been squandered, not just a casualty of war but a sacrifice to the Army's lack of preparedness. Empty shell holes stretched on both sides of the main road.

He turned back toward his squad's former position when he heard voices. He peered into the gloom between two piles of rubble. A shadow stood. Sergeant Heintzman.

"Sergeant, where's the Lieutenant?" Bert asked of the dark shadow.

Heintzman thumbed over his shoulder as he walked from the gloom.

"I need to report." Bert started in the direction the sergeant had indicated. Heintzman blocked Bert's path and shook his head.

"You'll have to report to me, Cronwette." The Sergeant's voice was flat, his eyes shaded. "Biscombe is covering the lieutenant, now."

"Oh." Bert mumbled. For a moment he stood dazed at the impact. He turned back and fell in step behind the sergeant. "I's sorry to hear that, Sarge."

"At his age, he should have been in the back seat of his Dad's car trying to make out at some drive-in." The sergeant spat disgustedly. "Not at this hell hole getting his guts splattered all over some stinking mud wall."

"Is the others someplace?" Bert looked around in the empty gloom.

"Your squad?" Heintzman ignored Bert's question.

"Why, they's just three of us. One is walking wounded."

"That makes five of us. We are your they, Cronwette." Heintzman summed the situation up softly.

Bert summoned his squad's survivors. The four clustered around the sergeant and peered nervously into the surrounding darkness. They were fully alert to a fusillade of fire at any moment from an attacking enemy infantry.

"That tank column was probably part of an expected NKPA drive on Chungju, just west of here. I have to believe some infantry will follow soon. If so, we're at risk to stay here." Sergeant Heintzman paused only a moment, then continued. "We move east. From here it's nigh on to five miles till we reach rough country and no rice paddies. Once in the relative cover of the hills, we'll move southeast deeper into the hills and stay away from roads till we can find friendlies." He looked at the other bedraggled survivors and waited. No questions. "Let's load up, men. Cronwette, you bring up the rear. Keep an interval of about ten yards. No noise. NKPA ears may be all around."

A pitiful file straggled into the darkness. Near the edge of last light, Bert heard a static crackle from among the rubble that had been Andong.

"Blocker One. Blocker One. This is Blocker Home. Come in Blocker One. Give us your report."

From deep, deep within Bert's well of anger and disgust came a mixture of dust, bitterness, and sputum. He spat violently into the darkness. "Thar's your damned report."

ೞ   ೞ   ೞ

The trek from danger seemed to last ages in the darkness of a night which Bert was sure cloaked masses of enemy infantry. When Bert's nerves were about to shatter, Sergeant Heintzman called a break.

"A farmer's honey-wagon, here by the side of the road may not be the nicest smelling place but it'll provide some cover in case of an enemy patrol. Just spread out around the off-side of the wagon and try to cop a few zzs." Sergeant Heintzman sagged onto the ground.

Bert eased to a place near the sergeant. "Sarge, how come they sent us with no proper equipment to stop them North Koreans?"

"Pretty simple, really." The sergeant shrugged. "We have no proper arms or ammunition available in the Far East."

"Golly how can the army tell us to fight tanks with just machine guns and no anti-tank stuff?"

"Well, I know the 25th Division has some bigger stuff they've moved ashore to the east. I guess the cavalry is on the way." The sergeant sighed audibly.

"Is them First Cav guys equipped with anti-tank stuff?"

"No, I just meant that help is on its way. We've got to keep holding and trying as best we can till help arrives. By now big stuff must be on its way." Heintzman's voice slurred from fatigue.

"I hope they gets in high gear with the big stuff. Them tanks is some monsters."

"In the meantime we do the best we can with what we have. Look, who was your platoon sergeant?" the sergeant wanted to offer hope to the neophyte NCO.

"Sergeant First Class England," Bert answered.

"Hey, John is a damn good man. We went ashore together in '44." Heintzman's words perked a bit. "Look, Cronwette any time you get in a pinch just ask yourself what England would do." Heintzman managed to slowly finish his advice. "Just do what he would have done. You'll be okay."

Bert leaned back. Soon he heard the sergeant's steady breathing and began to succumb to his own exhaustion. He was partially lulled by the new thought of trying to remember his old sergeant's leadership.

Just before dawn's first light, the survivors moved on toward the nearby mountains and turned south on a path roughly parallel to the Han River. By day's first full light they had reached comparative safety among some of the ridges. Heintzman led them up a shallow draw to a small copse of pines. They then moved up out of the bottom of the draw. It proved a correct thing to do since it rained later that day and the draw became a small stream of run-off.

During three days of careful travel they had no food other than a pot of fermented cabbage in an abandoned hut, before they found friendlies. They hooked up with a Republic Of Korea Army (ROKA) unit with an American advisor.

ᏇᏇ   ᏇᏇ   ᏇᏇ

Captain Goines again shook Bert's shoulder. "Stand, Cronwette."

Bert blinked, jumped to attention in the hot stuffy courtroom.

"The Board having heard the testimony will now adjourn to consider the evidence," the law officer intoned.

Bert watched without emotion as the officers and one enlisted representative of the Board, followed by the law officer, filed from the room. Captain Goines, appointed defense, relaxed. He turned to the accused. "I have a question, Corporal."

"Yes, Sir." Cronwette's apparent lack of emotion and his resignation showed in the tone of voice and the slump of the shoulders. He remembered the barracks sergeant's response when Cronwette asked what to expect from the military court. "Not much. Hang your cowardly ass."

The young First Lieutenant from the Adjutant General's table called breezily to Goines. "Captain, I'm stepping out for coffee. Care for any?"

"We could both use a cup on your way back, Lieutenant. Black, thanks."

"Oh." The Captain's answer obviously surprised the lieutenant. A suggestion to bring coffee for an enlisted man was unexpected. He finally shrugged and continued on his way.

Goines eased into his chair at the defense table and turned to Cronwette. "I noticed you frequently looked at one of the officers. Do you know a member of the Board?"

The accused shrugged a thin shoulder and slouched further into his metal folding chair. His sweat drenched body stuck to his starched khakis and he squirmed a bit trying to ease the fabric of his uniform loose. Starched khakis, temperature of ninety-plus degrees, and no air in the stuffy room ruined any idea of a military appearance.

Three of the five press representatives, one from Associated Press (AP), walked out the back door of the courtroom seeking a break from the heat. One of the two press representatives remaining in the hot room fanned himself idly with a copy of the "Charges and Specifications" distributed earlier by the Law Officer. He stopped waving the paper and read the crisp military

11

language, again.

HEADQUARTERS
FOURTH ARMY
ORDERS DIRECTING GENERAL COURT
27 April 1954

ACCUSED: Cronwette, Bertram J., Corporal RA18-202-349

CHARGE: Violation of Uniform Code of Military Justice, Articles 104 and 105, respectively, Holding intercourse with the Enemy and Giving Aid and Comfort to the Enemy.

SPECIFICATION: With Reference to Article 104, the accused did, on two separate occasions, meet with and hold intercourse with representatives of the enemy. With Reference to Article 105, the accused did speak to other internees after consultation with the enemy, making statements favorable to the enemy.

APPOINTED BOARD OF OFFICERS FOR GENERAL COURT
    Colonel Rudyard K. Simpson, Presiding Officer.
    Lieutenant Colonel Roscoe P. Battencourt.
    Major Orlando J. Montoya.
    Captain Roland L. Smith.
    Captain Edward R. Tanner.
    First Lieutenant Brandon L. Bartles.
    Master Sergeant Herman L. Fenton.

APPOINTED OFFICERS OF THE COURT
    Major Tidwell F. Smathers, Law Officer.
    Second Lieutenant Wendell H. Lawson, Judge Advocate General Office.
    Captain Martin O. Goines, Defense

 CB CB CB

Just outside the courtroom, under the door's overhang, the three press representatives who thought it might be cooler outside, stood disappointed.

"God! Couldn't that damn Bird Colonel find an air conditioned place?" the AP representative complained as he loosened his shirt collar.

"Well, this is Fort Sam Houston, Texas. Maybe he couldn't find an unused room with air conditioning," offered the reporter from the "San Antonio Express."

"Hell, they have air conditioning all over this place. My AP credentials got me a room at the BOQ, and into the Officer's club for dinner last night. Both cool as a cucumber. They know what air conditioning is. Why not use it?"

"Your Service ran the story last week. Remember, a judge in Maryland who won't let a jury be comfortable?"

"A jury?" The AP man took a drag on his cigarette. "Wait. I do remember, now. Juries, committees, and board meetings take longer if comfortable. But, why rush a bunch of officers? That poor clod's life is at stake."

"No. That article of the Uniform Code of Military Justice he's being tried under doesn't allow death. Life is the maximum allowed," the "Express" reporter reminded them.

"That's an alternative?" A harsh laugh came from the exasperated AP man.

"Seems to have been so for that lieutenant, this morning."

"Wasn't that a pisser? 'I wish to be excused for cause, Sir,'" mimicked the AP reporter.

"Oh, you mean the other returned POW, his attitude is understandable. He was also captured by the Chinese, but opposite of this corporal, the lieutenant was awarded the Congressional Medal for his organization and leadership of resistance."

"He spoke out didn't he? 'It is my opinion, Sir, with due respect to the court, the little coward should be hung, summarily,'" dramatized the newspaper reporter.

"I still don't get the jury bit?" complained the AP Man.

"The judge had court costs in mind. He knew that, say a case wraps up at two in the afternoon and the jury goes to a nice air conditioned room with big stuffed swivel chairs, the deliberations drag on as they enjoy their comfort. First thing you know the court has to pay for their dinner. That leads to the court having to pay for these guys in a motel for the night, breakfast, then some more comfort."

"Oh, I get it. If they're hot, sweaty, and miserable, they'll hurry up and make a decision just to get out."

"What's that got to do with this case? This Colonel doesn't have to pay the bill."

"He's a career man. Has a vested interest in the Army looking good to the taxpayers. A quick decision will look clear-cut, punishment for one sour apple, and no nonsense. For the folks at home it'll look good." The newspaper man made a quick reminder in his note pad.

"Hell, the way the press is digging the army about that general flying that GI from New Jersey around in the General's plane; Senator McCarthy screaming about Reds in the Pentagon; the army has to look tough."

"But, the Colonel in there is the ranking officer. Not one of the officers is gonna tell him to hurry up or slow down," the reporter from San Antonio added.

"I'll make you a bet. Your odds, Cronwette will get life, and if known, the Colonel will lead the vote. and, don't ask why but I'm betting on a quick decision and life." The AP man sadly shook his head.

Ɡ Ɡ Ɡ

"Do you know a member of the Court?" Goines repeated his question to Cronwette.

Cronwette slowly moved his head from side to side, his memory not focused on Captain Goines. His gaze held on the floor of the hot stuffy courtroom as if he were seeing thousands of miles and more then three years into his past. Having watched the remembered officer, his thoughts took him back to another hot day. A very hot day in the village of Hadong.

It had been hot that morning when they dismounted from the dusty and uncomfortable army trucks. The squads had formed for the two-mile march to their jumping-off point. The ever present stench from the paddies on both sides of the small rutted road stuck deep in the gut. One of the new squad members cleared his throat.

"If that gets rid of the smell, let me know." Bert smiled at the other uncomfortable GI.

"Gee, Corporal, I thought an old hand like you would be use to it?"

"I don't think you ever get used to it." As he spoke, Bert looked back at the squad strung along both sides of the road. Two GIs near the rear were side by side, talking.

"Keep your interval back there. Spread out."

"Those two are from the same hometown, Corporal."

"They'll be in the same body bag if them North Koreans drop a mortar in either one of their hip pockets."

They trudged along through the fine silt of the road dirt in silence. A row of hills on either side of the few paddies on the valley floor seemed to hold the heat and stench to the road. A never-ending sun beat down on their helmets. The GI across from Bert mopped under his helmet with his fatigue sleeve then looked up.

"Hey, Corporal, what outfit is this?"

Bert studied the young face a minute shrugged. "They don't name a provisional unit like us."

"But most of us are 187th Rifle Combat Team. We got off the boat from Okinawa yesterday."

"Well, the Army gets all wrapped up in attacks and don't worry 'bout keeping a regular unit if they need a bunch of men in a hurry. They just pull enough men and officers together and call it a provisional unit."

"What was your unit, Corporal?"

"In Japan I was with the 32d Regiment then put in a new outfit called Task Force Smith. It's made up of different units of the 24th Division. Then at Andong, the put my squad with some of the 25th

Division. Then they sent us over here. Unit names don't mean a thing to the army."

"What happened to that Smith thing?"

"The North Koreans beat the shit out o' us."

"How did you do at, that other place, you said with the 25th, Corporal?" Another curious and anxious GI chimed in.

"A bunch of T-34 tanks went through us faster than a dose of salts through a hired man," Bert replied quietly.

It was quiet awhile before one of the new GIs said anything. Finally a voice behind Bert asked the question on all their minds.

"Well, what's going to happen up where we're going, now?"

"A lot is going to depend on that captain of yours, the quartermaster captain. It'll depend a lot on if he knows how to fight a company."

"Hell, Corporal. He's not with us. Only that Lieutenant and the two sergeants are from our RCT."

Bert turned to question the GI about the Captain and noticed the GI pulled out his canteen. "I'd go easy on that water. The army is real short on keeping promises like getting food, water, and ammo up to troops."

Bert turned eyes to the front and shook his head. Damn! What a mess. Going into an attack with no heavy weapons, little ammo, GIs all strangers, no artillery. To top it off an officer in charge nobody knows, and the officer wearing quartermaster brass. Shit!

ଔ   ଔ   ଔ

Just the day before, Captain Roscoe P. Battencourt walked in the door of a Korean school house near Taejon. He automatically straightened his tie when he saw a sign, "24th Div HQ." The corridor was a buzz of activity. GIs and officers shuttled to and from various rooms. One GI in a rumpled uniform lay huddled in one corner. Asleep the captain hoped.

A sergeant first class came quickly along the hall. Battencourt raised a hand, "Where will I find G-3?"

A finger pointed to an open door was all the answer offered to the captain.

16

Battencourt looked at the indicated door then turned back to upbraid the sergeant for lack of military courtesy. The sergeant was already out of sight.

Inside G-3 was a babble of talk by groups of officers and men gathered around wall maps, field telephones, and tables. Some tables were upended ammo boxes. The nearest ammo-desk was occupied by a tired looking First John (First Lieutenant). Battencourt stopped in front of the first lieutenant and cleared his throat. He made a second attempt before the weary lieutenant looked up.

"May I help you, Sir?"

"I was given a note on the tarmac to report here. Battencourt." The captain handed the note to the lieutenant.

"Oh, yes, glad to see you, Captain. We need you to lead a provisional company attack on a village." He looked down at a map then continued. "Hadong, just east of here." He offered a weak smile.

"There must be some mistake." Battencourt straightened a bit as he renounced the idea.

"Oh no, Sir. No mistake. You are R. Battencourt, Captain, O23 471 203?"

"I am," Battencourt put a finger under his collar's brass quartermaster insignia, "But I'm no dumb foot-slogger and I am not leading a damn infantry operation."

"But, Sir..."

"Just a minute." The voice from behind Battencourt was gruff, loud, and a bit strained.

Battencourt rounded to give grief and faced a surprise in the form of a tall officer, gray at the temples, dark under the eyes, ramrod straight, and sporting silver eagles on his collar.

"I am a dumb foot-slogger, and you will lead the provisional company or I will convene the court martial for disobedience of a direct order in a combat zone. I have enough officers here to convene a court and enough under arms to execute the sentence." The tall colonel looked down from his six-inch greater height and riveted Battencourt with his glare.

"Oh no, I...I was just surprised at the order. I just..."

"Stand fast, Captain, I understnd." The colonel slumped a bit perceptibly. "You just got off the courier plane from Japan. You don't know infantry from Adam's off ox, and you're here on temporary duty to make an inventory of supply problems." A sigh from the softened colonel, "But we need a warm body with at least a captain's bars. You're here."

"Well, of course, Sir." Battencourt struggled to get on the best footing possible after his ill-advised remonstrance. "I was just quite surprised, Sir."

"I'm sure." The colonel beckoned Battencourt to follow as he walked to a wall map. On his way behind the colonel, Battencourt eagerly checked to insure his shirt was properly tucked in at the waist, and worked a shirt cuff over his belt buckle to get an acceptable luster.

After a thorough description of the land, the plan, and the fact that leading the individual units were a first john, a sergeant, and two corporals, all veterans, the colonel summed up.

"Look, Captain, all you need to do is stand aside, let the veterans run the show while you sit on a hill and watch a display as the troops take Hadong from a small platoon of North Korean Militia." The colonel smiled, "Hell, if I had a cushion I'd let you take it to sit on."

The Quartermaster Captain collected the company where the trucks left them. They marched from the drop-off to the assembly point. In clipped words he outlined the task. His strained words underscored his nervous fright.

"G-3 has designated this company to attack a platoon of enemy militia holding Hadong. The lieutenant's element will attack along this road. The second element will attack over the hill to your rear."

"Sir?" Bert was worried.

"Corporal?"

"Sir, them North Koreans might have an outpost on that hill. I could take a section up, kinda quiet-like and get rid of them."

"Sir, Sergeant Warton here, his idea may be a good one." Sergeant Warton was also fresh from the Task Force Smith debacle.

Captain Battencourt knew if he allowed a discussion of tactics it would undermine his command. He squared his shoulders and rejected tersely, "No questions allowed. We follow Division plans."

The other element of the small force began its movement along the road. Bert's unit slogged along the rice paddy dike to the foot of the target hill.

Sergeant Wharton eased next to Bert and spoke in a quiet voice. "Watch yourself and your men. Stay low. That Tight-Ass will get us all killed." Then the sergeant suggested, "Take the point and try to sneak a look-see."

Near the crest of the hill, Bert eased to the prone from his point position and bellied forward to look over the area. The top of the hill was an acre of near flat terrain. Few stunted pines grew in a small clump near one edge. On the opposite side he saw what he expected. An outpost of four enemy soldiers.

Intent on the outpost, Bert jumped when the Captain kicked his foot.

"Let's go, Corporal."

"Sir, they's a enemy look-out there," Bert whispered.

"All right, form the men and we'll run them off the hill."

"Well I can do it more quiet by sneaking 'round. Don't want to alert them enemy down in the village." Bert tried to reason.

"Corporal, I'm sick and tired of your interruptions." The Captain straightened his tie. "Form the men for assault."

The captain's "John Wayne-type" attack worked. It proved the U. S. had guessed wrong again. At the first noise the veteran outpost fired a few shots and scuttled down the hill into Hadong. The outpost had served its purpose. The veteran enemy platoon of T-34 tanks and attached infantry company went to full alert. The captain's assault had turned Hadong into a stepped-on ant hill.

Two tanks, each supported by a squad of infantry, rumbled onto the road, one in each of the two directions. The U. S. attack element on the road was in for a rude surprise. Bert anxiously watched an enemy skirmish line form at the base of his hill.

Bert and the other veteran NCO galvanized the small unit into action. They pushed the men to dig rifle pits along the hill's edge in preparation for the expected enemy barrage from the tanks in the village followed hard by infantry.

Disturbing thoughts and bitter memories of the previous defeat at Andong crowded Bert's thinking. How surprised and frightened he was when old rifle grenades did not explode. The panic Bert remembered when the enemy tanks demolished the village unmolested. His anguish when desperate calls for artillery counter-battery fire on a radio too weak to broadcast over the Korean Hills went unanswered.

Unfit and inexperienced officers like this Captain pushed into command, more rattled and less aware of what actions to take than the men they were supposed to lead.

The present situation came back to the fore of his thinking. How should he anchor his line of rifle pits on this hill? He had no heavy or light machine guns, not even a good Browning Automatic Rifle. Should he call for fixed bayonets now? Okay, he remembered to ask himself, what would Sergeant England do?

The first shell of the North Korean barrage startled the Captain. He jumped at the explosion. Shocked, he screamed at Bert. "Enemy artillery!"

The captain ran to the crest of the hill and looked down the long rugged slope. The enemy skirmish line started up. He could easily imagine each enemy skirmisher aimed at him personally. The quartermaster captain struggled for composure.

"We have to abandon the hill," called the Captain.

"No, we gotta dig in." Bert screamed.

Bert knew the unit assault by road would need this unit on the hill to keep the enemy from turning their full force up the road. "Them guys on the road need us to dig in and keep them Gooks busy," he pointed out.

The Captain ran along the crest of the hill, wildly waved his arms and screamed, "No. Division was wrong. We can't stay."

Bert and the other NCO kept the men working amid the enemy barrage.

"Dig."

"Hurry up, dig deep."

"Keep it moving."

Another shell burst just below the hill's crest. The Captain screamed. Eyes wide, he ran past the line of lathered and worried riflemen.

"C'mon, Men," Bert called. "We can do it. We'll hold 'em."

Clods of hard dirt settled in front of the rifle pits in the making. One GI paused to mop his face. "Hey, Randy, what about that corporal?"

"I don't know him."

"But you were talking with him. What's he like?" The GI renewed his assault on Korea with another hard swing of his entrenching tool.

"He seems all right. He went in with Task Force Smith."

"I hear they got their asses kicked." Randy's friend protested.

"But he knew enough to survive, didn't he?"

"Let's hope he knows what he's doing, then. I wanna walk off this damn hill."

"If he can get us off in one piece, I'm with him." The GI looked at the retreated Captain just skirting the back of the hill. "I sure can't count on that stupid shit. Flopping around like a chicken with his damn head cut off."

CB   CB   CB

Stay they did. The green filler troops of the Rifle Combat Team, fresh from Okinawa, were scared. No more scared than Bert but to them he was an old hand, a knowledgeable veteran. He had survived a battle. In their eyes he would know what to do. Unsure that they had any future other than a few short minutes left to live on this forsaken hill, the veteran had said, "We will."

Bert Cronwette was not a commanding military presence. Thin and emaciated when released from the POW camp he would not have weighed more than one-hundred-fifty on the hill at Hadong. Maybe more than one-fifty if you counted his basic weapon also. Tall, skinny, angular, wearing fatigues he had slept in and worn for three weeks, he looked shaggy and drooped, big time.

The green troops rallied to his leadership and fighting will. They stayed. Bert moved along the firing line quickly after each assault. He tried to remember all Sergeant England said about a defense perimeter. Always keep the best interval between rifles pits.

Bert's eyes, recessed under prominent sinus bulges, gave him an eerie look as he prowled his section of the line into the gathered dark. When the other NCO was wounded, Bert prowled both sections of the line. He moved riflemen from any pit where two men lay if a nearby pit was vacant of living. Sergeant England always warned a vacant rifle pit made an open door to an attack element. To fight an enemy in your front was bad. To have them infiltrate and attack from both front and rear was suicide.

As dark descended, Bert scooted flankers to both sides of the hill and sent a rear guard to the back of the hill.

He remembered Sergeant England. "Always keep your back door open."

The green GIs relied on Bert as he controlled the line. They did not know that his efforts to make radio contact with the other unit were unsuccessful. They held the hill through a night of bayonet and rifle assaults.

The night brought no rest for Bert. After each assault, he scouted the line, moved men where needed and encouraged.

"How we doin' here?"

"Lookin' good, men."

"Them Gooks gonna back off soon."

"Fire at sure targets. Don't go wastin' ammo."

"Keep diggin' that foxhole deeper. Don't stop workin'."

The wounded NCO was moved to the back of the line bandaged. In one of the later assaults, Bert received a flesh wound. Sulfa powder and a bandage sufficed.

As the sky to the east begin to show dull gray light, Bert scouted the NKPA. They were not formed for a renewed attack. With no food and nearly out of ammo, Bert moved his men off the hill. Bert's count was six killed (KIA) and four wounded (WIA). He moved his survivors and the casualties east into the new day's light.

Bert did not see the Captain again in Korea. The quartermaster officer was, in the words from a song by Hank Snow, popular at the time, "Short-coupled and long-gone."

The Captain had bugged out.

Chapter 2

Who is Bert?

The older woman sat in the noisy, hot, clutter, and dust of the office. She brushed up a possibly out-of-place strand of hair on her forehead. A moment later her other hand fluttered to a stand of gray that may have come loose from the tight bun at the nape of her neck.

The door to the inner office opened unexpectedly and she started. The record book in her lap plopped onto the floor. She quickly retrieved it and looked up.

"Okay, Miss Lewiston, go on in."

The frail woman eased into the office. Inside, a stocky man sat behind a battered desk strewn with papers and dust.

"Close the door."

She did.

"Sit."

Again, she complied after making a quick, compulsive swipe at any possible dust on the seat of the chair.

The mill superintendent worked on his paper pad a few minutes longer, laid down his pen, and looked at the Mill School's one teacher.

"End-of-year reports?"

She quietly handed them across the desk.

"Failures?"

"Yes, one, sir."

"Don't tell me," he sighed. "Cronwette."

She cleared her throat nervously and answered affirmatively.

"Well," the superintendent leaned back and sighed. "I guess it's been all the school can do for that dummy. With his dad's accident last month, there's no mill worker in that mill house. Don't want to move Madge Cronwette out on the road." He paused again, sighed once more and continued. "How old is Bert, now?"

"Just past fifteen, sir," quite relieved that she was not considered the cause of a failure on the mill school's record.

"Okay, God knows you did your best. Let's put him to work."

ఴ ఴ ఴ

At Maw's call, Bert shrugged into his worn denim overalls. Cut down from his Paw's old overalls, they were thread-bare to start. He climbed down from his loft and trundled sleepily to the outhouse. Once relieved, Bert returned to the small cabin.

"Morning, Maw."

"Son." Maw was not known for long-winded conversations.

Bert moved past his Maw, picked a tin cup from a shelf, and poured coffee from the pot of boiled brew on the stove. Bert carefully poured part of the coffee onto a small saucer. Cradled up to his lips, the saucer of coffee was in position to be cooled. He blew softly and sipped.

Maw had put an old chipped plate on the table. Bert took two lard biscuits from the skillet and ladled gravy over them. He sipped his saucered coffee again and started breakfast.

"What'd you cut this coffee with, Maw?"

"Is it all right?"

"Ain't bad."

"Found some chicory and dried it. Gotta cut where we can, Bertie"

"Know, Maw."

Maw poured a bit of the coffee in her tin cup onto a saucer, blew, and sipped.

"Not a bad mix at that. Makes that five cent a pound coffee at the Mill Store go a piece further." She paused for another sip. "Save all we can."

"Yes, Maw."

Bert sopped the last of his gravy, stuffed two biscuits into the bib pocket of his overalls and left for work.

At the mill, Bert was a hard worker. Relieved from the deep hurt of his failures at school and not saddled with written instructions, he worked well. Pay wasn't all that good. Every payday there were the Mill's deductions for house rent, groceries charged that week at the Mill Store, and breakage. Money left, if any, was given in cash. Maw tried any way she could to keep the grocery charges down.

By the end of the second year of work at the Mill, Bert began to worry. He learned his job well, but, was that to be all there was to his life? The next forty years or so in the dirt and noise of the mill?

The answer to Bert's questioning came one fateful Sunday afternoon. After he and Maw walked back from the Sunday Church Service, she sent Bert to the store. Maw wanted to cook a kettle of beans for the next week and needed a bit of fatback for flavoring.

At the Mill Store a group of other workers were sitting on the porch listening to a soldier tell about the war and the army. The soldier had worked at the Mill before he was drafted back in 1942. He was visiting the "Old Gang" and spinning a few war stories.

One of the fellows called Bert over. The soldier bragged about his great life now with no war.

"Hell, sit on my butt, mostly." He stretched languidly, smiled and leaned back in his chair.

"Don't got no marching or things?" Oscar the saw-setter at the Mill asked.

"Oh, once in a while, Saturdays mostly, we have to do a parade and inspection."

"That all?"

"Well, if'n it's still close enough to pay day, then we head into town."

Slim, Bert's partner on the cutting machine, elbowed Bert and grinned, "Get drunk."

"Like a skunk. Find me a woman whose bed I can share."

Slim stamped a foot. "Hot damn."

The soldier basked in the envy of his old mill friends. He smiled and continued. "One fella says soldiering is just drinkin', fuckin', and throwing money away."

The soldier's stories captivated Bert. Three full meals each day. Free clothes, a bed, and pay. Bert did wonder one point. With his lack of experience he couldn't understand, if the soldier had a bed, why go to town and give some of his money to some woman to sleep in her bed?

After considerable thought and callow deliberation, Bert wanted a chance to learn more about the army. A month later his chance came. The mill closed for a day of repairs and maintenance. Bert hitched a ride to the nearest town of any size and walked around 'till he found the Army Recruiting Office.

Bert walked in the door. A man in an army uniform sat at a battered metal desk about half-way back of the hot room. A fan labored in one corner but seemed to only make noise, stir very little dust, and no air.

The sergeant looked up from his desk and saw a tall, lanky kid looking at him from under a thatch of tousled hair. The overalls the kid wore were patched and worn at the cuffs. The denim shirt must have been homemade or a hand-me-down roughly altered by hand. The shoulder seams were crooked. Shoes were badly scuffed and run over at the heels. One shoe lace was broken and tied in a knot to allow continued wear.

"Afternoon, young fellah. Hot 'nuff?"

Recruiting Sergeant First Class Donald Woodruff prided himself on being able to talk 'back home,' to potential recruits. He figured most of them came fresh from some cane break. He wanted to make them feel at home.

"Yes, Sir. It's a mite warm."

"Well, come on in the house and sit a spell."

Sergeant Woodruff smiled, pointed to the only unoccupied chair and sized up the potential recruit. Whatever cane break this one was from looked to be a damn poor cane break. From the looks of the skin and bones, this one probably never had three meals in one day in his life.

"How can I help you, young man?"

"Well...ah...I's told the Army's a good deal."

"Damn right. Somebody told you the truth. What part of that good life do you want me to talk about?"

"Well, soldiers get paid, regular like?"

"Yes, sir. Once a month. They get sixty dollars a month to start. That's rain or shine." The sergeant held up his hand and counted on his fingers as he extolled the further wonders. "Plus, three square meals each and every 365 days of the year. Free uniforms, head to foot. Free laundry. Free bed to sleep in, and a roof over your head." Even though this was part of the Bible Belt, Woodruff added, "Cheap beer at the enlisted men's club."

"Gosh."

Woodruff pulled a form from his desk and while Bert goggled at the offered luxuries, began to ask questions and fill in blanks. That completed he pulled out a copy of the Armed Forces Qualification Test. "Now, this is a test. You said you finished grade eight, this will be a breeze."

Woodruff then glanced at the latest memo from the Recruiting District Office. The memo had criticized him for not meeting his last quota. With that indictment in mind and his evaluation of it as unjustified, Sergeant Woodruff added, "Any of those questions difficult or don't make sense, just let me know. We can work it out."

It was not unknown for a recruiter facing a difficult quota imposed by headquarters, to help recruits. This recruiter was hurting to meet his quota.

Eighteen? Yes.

Sound of body? Yes.

Know which is your right hand? Yes.

Test score at least minimum? Yes. (Saw to that.)

Welcome to the U. S. Army!

Maw moved her meager possessions into a small room in her sister's house near Memphis and paid her rent with Bert's military dependent's allotment.

⚃ ⚃ ⚃

Bert was not impressed at his first sight of the basic training area. To Bert, raised among thick stands of conifers, the large expanses of waving grass and bare open hills presented a strange sight. Not many trees and those looked stunted.

He was issued a mattress, bedding, and assigned a cot in the barracks. As long as Bert could remember he had slept on an old blanket in a loft of the mill cabin.

At his first army meal, Bert was astounded. He had heard of sliced white bread but here it was. All he had to do was eat. Milk in big pitchers. All kinds of food, some new to Bert, all on his own tray.

A new world opened to Bert. All the food he could eat three times each day. He was given more clothes than he and Maw owned even if he counted some of Paw's old clothes. It was like the soldier at the Mill Store said, training was fun, new people to meet, and he learned about all the different weapons. He did miss his old bib overalls though. The NCOs wouldn't let him stuff things in his fatigue jacket pockets. All in all, he still liked his new life.

After basic training and a couple of weeks leave, he was sent overseas to Japan. This was a part of a new life to which Bert looked forward.

The plan for the use of troop ships in peace time accommodated four classes of people. The sailors who crewed the ship had their own quarters, much like crew quarters on most other surface ships operated by the Navy. The few Army personnel, since this was essentially an Army activity, had their separate quarters. The passengers consisted of the remaining two groups. Officers and civilian dependents traveled in the various compartments above deck and ate in a dining room in the upper deck area. Enlisted personnel in transit were quartered below deck in large compartments.

The word large by no means indicated spacious, or roomy for the individual. The space was large by dimensions, some 50 by 20 feet, and quartered some 150 humans, all enlisted in beds 3 by 6 feet consisting of rough canvas tied inside a metal frame and stacked two feet apart between deck and overhead.

Bert had no time to get seasick, at least not the first six days. He was on KP.

"KP," rumbled the big master sergeant as he glared at the hapless KPs, who fresh from eight weeks basic training, were still convinced that sergeants were cast, not born, stood quietly. The big burly character said, "KP means your ass belongs to me all day. For the next six days you get your lazy asses in here when I say. You don't slack till I say to."

As punctuation, the mess sergeant glared individually at each GI. Then, with a thin smile, he said. "You get your lazy asses in here on time, work like I tell you. We ain't got no trouble."

After a pause, possibly to catch his wind, the sergeant continued. "Them of you as want to goof off, go ahead. Warn you now, you goof off and I'll stick on your ass worse than stink on shit."

A group of three ship's crew sat at a table in the far corner of the Mess Deck and snickered in their coffee cups. As regular crew, they had probably heard the same routine twice each voyage. For them the best was to come.

"Now, I don't asks the impossible. You ain't gotta polish no turd. Just do your job, as I tell you."

The mess sergeant glared at the eleven and Bert for a minute then said, "Questions?"

Not a sound.

"Next, Short Arm Inspection."

A giggle burst from the three swabbies.

The mess sergeant ignored the sailors and raised an index finger. "I ain't having no dripping yardbirds on my Mess Deck."

"Just stand in line where you are." he continued. "Unbutton your pants and pull it out. When I come to you, give it a squeeze, milk it down, and stand at ease."

As a line of red-faced GIs stood the Army's standard short arm inspection in quiet embarrassment, the swabbies, snickered, nudged one another, and generally exhibited their glee.

After the second night of KP, Bert decided to take a shower. He almost stepped into the slop on the floor of the latrine before he saw the cesspool. The doors on a ship do not go to the floor. The door is a metal cover for an opening through which people pass. The bottom of the door opening is six inches above the floor. The water from plugged commodes sloshed around in the six inches of enclosed space. Paper shreds, human waste, and other bits of waste floated in the slop.

Bert slept dirty for the rest of the voyage.

There was one other problem for Bert. On KP was also a loudmouth from Appalachia. The guy complained, groused, and as Bert said, "Carped like he's the biggest carp in a small pond."

What does a GI do on a troop ship if not on KP? Bert didn't know. He spent his first day off KP trying to find out. He loafed on deck; tried to find a useable latrine; loafed on deck; and searched in vain for a useable latrine.

The second day after KP was over, he went on deck to be greeted by cold winds. One of the other GIs said the ship was on some kind of Great Circle Route from Seattle to Yokohama. That route put the ship close to the Aleutian Islands for a day or two. Wind from the North Pacific swept stark and cold across the deck.

He sought warmth below deck. Bert remembered a stairway next to the door to the Mess Deck. It led up to the next deck but was blocked at the top by a heavy metal grill. Bert found it warmer sitting on those stairs. He was comfortable enough to begin getting drowsy.

"We're more than half way."

Bert jumped and looked around. No one.

Then, from above the grill, "Less than six days to go."

Bert looked up through the grill and realized the deck above was the dining room for officers and dependents. The clink of glasses, china, and flatware floated down the stairway. Occasional bits of conversation drifted down with the other sounds.

"Your husband has been stationed where?"

"Some kind of special Advisory Group."

"Would that be in Korea?"

"Yes, a Kay, something."

"Korea is a very backward country."

"In one letter he said we'd live near the Korean capitol but that in a year, we'd transfer to Tokyo."

"Much better living."

"You've been to Tokyo?"

The crowd of GIs that line up early for chow began crowding into the passage below Bert's perch near the door to the Mess Deck. The conversation from the deck above was inaudible. Bert wondered as he got into the chow line about being stationed in a backward country. He hoped he'd be stationed in a modern country.

The boredom of the next day and the cold winds kept Bert below decks again. Late in the morning he sought his warm perch on the stairwell. This time out of curiosity, Bert edged closer to the grill. Not much more was visible; a corner of one table with a cloth table cover; one small round window with curtains on it.

He again dozed only to be awakened by the increased murmur of activity above. Conversation buzz. Glasses and china clattered. People came to the table above Bert's perch and he slid down a step or two.

"I'll be at Itazuki, 24th Division Headquarters."

"Oh, I thought you said earlier that first assignments were made by GHQ after arrival?"

"A friend at G-1, Pentagon, wangled me a direct assignment."

"Then you don't go through GHQ?"

Bert was amazed that right above him was an officer so important that he got a special assignment. He moved up to the grate and moved different ways but could not see this important officer.

"Why is it so special to have a command in a field division?"

"I can add this to my resume if I want to get a job after retirement. A regimental command will be impressive. Look good."

"Oh, you're a combat veteran. You've had command experience?"

"Well, no war command."

"But what if there is a war?

"European Command is where a war will be. Russians won't start a war in Japan."

Chow call interrupted Bert. He jumped down. He was hungry.

32

Bert came out of pipeline, ready for his assignment in this new world when the ship tied up to the pier in Yokohama. Now arrived in Far East Command, Bert was assigned 32d Regiment, 24th Division, Eighth United States Army, Japan.

Bert and fourteen other new arrivals climbed into the back of a large army truck the morning after their arrival in Japan. For two days the hapless GIs bounced south in the back of the open truck. Bert found the first part of the journey interesting because of its newness. People, houses, trees, and all were wonders to Bert.

The truck deposited the tired green troopers at the front of a low two-story wooden structure. Stiff, weary, and dirty they dismounted with the duffel bags they had used as pillows the previous nights. After collecting the trash from the C-rations they had enjoyed during the trip, they stood, stretched, and looked around. Their new home was part of a vast compound of similar structures that had once been a Japanese Army Compound.

A young corporal appeared from the building, called roll, led them up a wide stairs, down a long hall, and into a squad room at the end of the hall. Fifteen iron bunks crowded the room. They began to choose bunks and ground their duffels.

"Attention!"

All turned in the direction of the command and assumed the required position. The sergeant first class who had barked the command stood at attention and looked straight ahead.

The sergeant was of medium height and carrying no fat under his closely tailored fatigues. Those fatigues were starched and pressed into sharp creases. Two of the sharp creases went through the exact vertical center of each breast pocket and continued in sharp profile the length of his fatigue trousers. Bert was soon to learn that his uniform and the others, was to be tailored and starched the same as the ramrod sergeant at all times.

Bert's view of the sergeant was interrupted by a taller and slimmer first lieutenant whose uniform was similarly creased and starched. The officer marched to the center of the room and called, "At ease."

The lieutenant strode briskly around the room, stopped briefly in front of each new squad member, and returned to a position near the door.

"Gentlemen, welcome to the Third Platoon, Love Company, 32d Regiment, 24th Division. During the next few weeks you will continue your basic training as an infantry squad. We will work as a unit learning more advanced tactics, both platoon and company. We are scheduled for field exercises in four weeks. You will be trained, hardened physically and mentally ready for those exercises by that time. During the exercises we will be evaluated and scored both as a unit and as individuals. Work will be with weapons, some new to you. We will have no live ammunition."

He viewed the men as he paused briefly, then continued. "I am Lieutenant Perry, your platoon leader. Do not hesitate to see me on any problem or concern you and Sergeant England, your squad leader, can't adequately handle. He's your next link in the chain of command pending selection of a new assistant squad leader."

Again the pause, mostly for effect, then, "Welcome to the 24th."

The newly formed squad worked with the 3.5 mm rocket launcher, called "Bazooka." During those weeks they cleaned, disassembled, reassembled, and dry-fired the 2.3 mm mortar, .30 caliber heavy water-cooled machine gun, and the .75 mm recoilless rifle.

Bert enjoyed the training as part of the U S Army of Occupation, Japan. He found it interesting to use new weapons, and enjoyed the easy life the soldier at the mill that Sunday had told him about. The first four weeks passed rapidly for Bert. Then, a notice was posted on the squad room bulletin board on a Friday afternoon.

"Squad assembly, 1800 hours."

The squad members were there at the appointed time. Sergeant England entered accompanied by the Company Clerk.

"Listen up, men. We've finished four weeks of training. We'll begin Monday with combined battalion activities. At this point you are going to be issued Class A passes."

He glared at the smiles and eager faces that seemed to blossom at the magic of the words Class A pass. The chatter quickly died under his frown and he continued.

"When Corporal Bronson calls each name you will come forward, sign for your pass, and you're free 'till 0500 hours, Monday."

He raised a hand to halt movement by a couple of over-eager GIs toward the Company Clerk.

"Hold on. Hear me and hear me good." Sergeant England paused to be sure he had every squad member's attention before he continued. "Each and every one is expected to be here in the squad room no later than 0500 hours each Monday through Saturday. You will not drag in here at 0505 hours. If you do, Class A privileges will disappear. You will not plan to leave the squad area any earlier than 1700 hours, Monday through Friday or 1300 hours on Saturday."

He paused to look each squad member in the eye.

"Further, there will be, from time to time, extra drills, inspections, and activities...GI parties, for example, requiring you to be here Class A Pass or no."

He paused, then, "Questions?"

Again he paused. No questions.

"Corporal, take over." The corporal began calling names. Sergeant England left the room, walked to a closed door near the center of the large wooden barracks building, and knocked.

At Lieutenant Perry's terse "Enter," England entered, closed the door to the Platoon Leader's small office. "Sergeant England reporting, Sir." England saluted and stood to attention.

"Have a seat, John," Perry returned the salute, smiled, and waved a hand toward the other straight chair. Part of Perry's smile was a greeting and part was the sure knowledge that he was lucky to have the sharpest NCO in the regiment as his platoon sergeant. England heartily agreed with Perry's concept of training that included physical toughness.

"I'd like your assessment of the potential of our newest squad." Perry paused then continued, "Would you see any of that squad as possible leadership material?"

"Well, off hand, Sir, I'd consider Cronwette as a likely prospect." England paused a brief moment before he summed his evaluation, "He may be a bit rough in his language but he's a good

35

head, learns fast, and does as told the first time, Sir."

"Okay. I share that assessment." The young platoon leader paused a minute, absently rubbed his chin, then added, "We'll keep our eyes on him during regimental exercises. Those ratings and evaluations will be important." After a moment in thought, Lieutenent Perry smiled, "Thanks, John."

The sergeant stood, saluted, about-faced, and left.

ଔ ଔ ଔ

The pleasures of soft garrison life in Japan began for the new squad members. One squad member immediately found a local lady with whom he set up housekeeping off base. A couple of the others left the base especially Saturday afternoon after the last inspection, to visit the local lovelies.

Bert seldom left the base. The food was good and abundant. Local indigenous personnel, many former soldiers in the Japanese Army, worked the kitchen. No KP for the GIs. Bert liked the army.

At the Post Exchange (PX), Bert met the loud-mouthed complainer from KP on the troop ship.

"Hey, Buddy, been on KP lately?"

"No KP but plenty of PT."

"Hell, we seldom work up a sweat. Haven't had any physical training in..." he made an exaggerated reach for his forehead as if scratching. "Why, I plumb forgot."

"We got one of them Gung ho lieutenants. He thinks we gotta be in shape for World War III," Bert responded a bit tiredly.

"Ouch. Well, gotta go. Support'n a moose and hooch, Old Buddy."

The guy in the squad with the live-in arrangement explained that moose was local GI slang for woman. Hooch was house, hut, or room.

Bert never bothered to run down for mail call like most of the squad. He got one letter from Maw, once. He was surprised when the orderly room clerk called him down the second time for a letter from Shirley Ann, a girl from home. He was more confused after he read the letter than he was surprised to get a letter from her.

Dear Berti,

I do miss you since we had fun 'fore you left. When is the army gonna let you come home from that Japan? I bet it's a susprise to you 'cause we gonna have a baby. I am so happy to be havin' your baby. Write and tell me when we gonna get married.

Now what was he to do? Emmy, a friend from the mill told him Shirley Ann was going to have Jock's baby. Should he write and tell her it's Jock's baby? Tell her he don't want to get married? He didn't know what to do? His mind constantly mulled the problem.

A week later, after evening chow, Sergeant England called to Bert, "Cronwette, I need to see you. In my room."

Bert entered the small cadre room, England motioned him to a chair and waited for Bert to sit down.

"Cronwette, you haven't been with it this last week. You've messed up on a couple of drills I didn't expect you to blow. Got a problem?"

Bert withered. His shoulders slumped forward and he cut his eyes down to his boots. "Well," he finally managed, "I been worried."

The Sergeant's voice and his face relaxed a bit, "Problems at home?"

"Yea, Sarge."

In a much friendlier tone England probed, "What's the girl's name?"

"Gee, how'd you know they's a girl?"

"Cronwette, I could buy Japan if I had a nickel for every GI who gets bad news from a girl back home." England smiled slightly in a rare and warmer way, and added, "Why don't you relax and tell me about this girl and the problem?"

"Well," Bert squirmed, unsure what to say, "It's kinda hard to start."

England waited a bit. A familiar routine for him and other squad and platoon leaders. Almost every week one of their members or another gets the proverbial "Dear John" or this, its

37

brother letter, "What about the baby?"

After a minute waiting for Bert, England added, "Look, Bert, I may not be the oldest wheel on the jeep but I've been through the mud a time or two. Tell me about her."

Unsure how to begin to explain it, Bert shrugged and handed Shirley's letter to Sergeant England.

"You sure it's okay for me to read it?"

Bert nodded his head slightly and sat, eyes downcast as England struggled through the letter best described as writing writing and not reading writing. When he finished working through the letter, England sat for a minute, eyes on the paper.

To the sergeant it was an old story. Not as final as the "Dear John" but more devastating because of the burden it placed on the callow. Cronwette was among the most callow.

"Okay. Tell me about this," England glanced down at the paper, again, "...this Shirley."

Bert began slowly to explain about the girl. How he had always thought she looked so fine. How at home on leave she had talked him into going for a walk in the woods.

"You had sex?"

"Yeah," still half embarrassed.

"That was the only time you had sex with her?"

"Gosh," he blurted to the Sergeant, "That's the first time I had any sex." Bert blushed more, looked down, and missed the momentary smile on England's lips.

"Well, had you and your girl talked about marriage?"

"Shucks, Sarge," Bert shrugged one frail shoulder. "I don't see as how she's my girl."

"Had you dated any before the night you had sex?"

"Naw."

"Okay, other than she likes to take virgins for a roll in the grass, what do you know about this girl?"

"Well, I know Shirley Ann is gonna have Jock's baby. Could she be having one atop the other, you know, two?"

"Two?"

"Yes, Sir, one by Jock and then a second on top 'cause of that night?"

38

"Wait. Jock's baby?" An old story seemed to be emerging. Sergeant England picked. "Who is Jock and how do you know it's his baby?"

"He's the mill foreman's big bully son. And, Widow Conley said the baby's Jock's"

"Widow Conley? Who is she, now?"

"Well, she's the midwife for folks at the mill."

Sergeant only took another minute to see the story, a plot older than Moses.

"Let's be sure I got this straight. Who's idea was it to go for a walk in the woods?" probed the sergeant.

"Shirley Ann."

"Who's idea to have sex under that tree?"

"It's real nice like." Bert looked straight at the sergeant and grinned a bit bashfully.

"I understand, but who had the idea first?"

"Shirley Ann."

"Who said anything about getting married?" prompted England, again.

"That's Shirley Ann."

Sergeant England leaned back in his chair and shook his head. "She's got more ideas than a Saturday night WAC on Sunday morning."

"Say what?"

"Never mind, Cronwette. And the midwife, says this is Jock's baby?"

"Sure."

"Could you think that this, Jock, won't own up so maybe this Shirley thinks you will come through with an allotment? You think she would do something like that?"

Bert was silent for a minute then sat up straight. "Yes, Sir. She just wants my money."

England reached over and patted Bert's shoulder. "Sure sounds like that to me."

"An' I don't have to get married?" The face beamed with the new idea.

"Why don't you just tear that letter into little pieces and flush it down the latrine?" England smiled, "Just ignore it and get back to being a good soldier. Let Shirley and Jock work out their own problem."

Bert felt instantaneous relief. He wanted the army and his life to stay just like it was. He didn't need a wife. The sex thing was real nice, but no wife.

Time passed. Bert continued to do well. He was a good and willing soldier, his scores on the target range were best in the company. Yes, life in the army was good for Bert.

Chapter 3

Army Games

Reveille came as usual for a Monday morning. Only the quick movement and hushed tones of the small talk in the latrines belied the unusualness. Once back from chow the squad stretched beds, adjusted dust covers to completely hide the pillow and some tested the tautness of the blanket for the third or fourth time with their own dime.

Satisfied with the barracks' condition against any inspection, they squirmed into field packs and adjusted web belts, first aid packs, and canteens.

"Hey, Bert," called Caparelli, "think they'll do inspections while we're in the field?"

"Can't say, but like Sarge says, be ready for the worst," Bert answered and from habit, before looking up, added, "Caparelli, turn around. Yep, canteen on wrong again." Bert quickly made the necessary adjustment to the attaching hooks and shook his head. "How'd you ever get through basic?"

Johnston, passing by said, "He really flunked basic, but since he was the only one in Fort Lost in the Wood's history, they let him go. That way the allotment for his organ grinder monkey was safe."

"Blow it, Johnston," Caparelli fumed. The sergeant's whistle shrilly broke the chatter.

The men jog-stepped from the barracks and fell into formation quickly. Each knew his place and who was to be on his right, left, front, and rear.

Sergeant England called, "Attention!" then proceeded to adjust file and rank positions from the head of each file. Routine

41

completed, he returned to the platoon sergeant's position and saluted platoon leader, Lieutenant Perry.

"All present or accounted for, Sir."

Perry returned the salute. "Thank you, Sergeant. Post."

As England marched to the platoon sergeant's position at formation, Perry ordered, "At ease."

After a second's hesitation, Perry addressed the platoon.

"Gentlemen, we will be in the field for most of the week. Your conduct as soldiers will be observed as will the cadre's. We will be evaluated and marked by a team from Division HQ. I expect your conduct to be exemplary and the resulting report to be a commendation."

He paused and looked over the platoon before continuing, "I expect each man to do his best, do it sharply, and prove to Division that this platoon is the best in Far East Command."

"Attention!" With the platoon at the position the lieutenant continued. "Sergeant England, take the platoon to its bivouac."

Once marched out of the immediate compound and on the main road through the base, the platoon swung along, it's formation held well, and the GIs looked good. From the rear of the marchers came Lieutenant Perry's call, "The best platoon in the 24th Division is on the road, Sergeant England. Time to let folks know the best is up and marching."

First came the strong cadence commands.

"Hup, two, threep, four. Pick it up, men. Left, right, left."

Bert felt a surge of pride as the footfalls sounded as one large boot that thudded onto the road with each call.

"Your left, right, left. Your left." Pause. "Your left. Count cadence, count."

The platoon responded:

"One, two, three, four."

"One, two," a silent beat then the rushed "threefour."

"Once more," England called, "and sound off like you had two."

The platoon again responded straining for the lusty sound.

"One, two, three, four.

One, two," silent beat, "threefour."

"All right, men, this platoon and Jodie'll wake 'em up." England's voice dropped into a rich baritone and the ballad began.

"You had a good home and you left." he called.

"You're right." The platoon response was with the fall of the right foot.

"Your girl was there when you left." England called.

"You're right." Again the platoon.

"Jodie was there when you left." England's voice was deep, rich. Bert listened enviously to the rousing sounds.

"You're right." The platoon.

"Ain't no use of going home. . .Jodie's got your girl and gone." England sang the World War II marching ballad.

"Am I right or wrong?"

"You're right." The platoon responded.

"Am I right or wrong?"

"You're right." Again, the platoon.

Bert's feelings were high. A strong affinity with the squad, platoon, and England swelled in Bert. He struggled to suppress a laugh of sheer pleasure he had never felt before. Goose-bumps covered both arms. This was life, comradeship, and belonging. God it felt good.

"I don't know but I been told,

This platoon is good as gold."

Am I right or wrong?" England led.

"You're right."

"Am I right or wrong?"

"You're right."

Bert didn't think how many others in the squad had the same feelings. He was captivated by the march. Bert did not have a conscious evaluation of his emotions at that time. It was, however the first time in his life he felt of himself as belonging, as being not just one but he thought of himself as part of something bigger.

And so for the first two miles, the cadence was maintained by one or the other of the three squad leaders as the platoon swung through route step. For the last switchback in the road up the mountain the cadence was dropped as the steeper climb broke the step. Near the bivouac area, England called a halt briefly to allow

43

dressing the formation.

Lieutenant Perry called for attention and marched the platoon into the area. The Division inspection team watched the platoon's arrival. Packs were grounded in the assigned area as Sergeant England set two pegs in the ground. With these pegs as guides, the platoon soon had each GI's individual shelter half connected one to the other, and the resulting two-man tent, front peg aligned with the two pegs set by England, were erected in short order.

The designated areas for the slit trenches were selected, dug, and the platoon was in shape when the other platoons arrived. Bert smiled with some pride in his platoon as he watched the other platoons struggle with the simple process to connect the two halves of the individual shelter halves, put tent poles together, drive in pegs, and pull tent ropes taut. Bert began to understand the value of Lieutenant Perry's drive. Bert's platoon marched sharply, set up bivouac quickly, and prepared for the field exercise crisply. The other platoons, with platoon leaders less demanding than Perry, had trouble erecting their tents, and when erected formed a ragged line. Quite a bit of the morning was spent by all other platoons in aligning tents, digging latrine ditches, and getting organized properly.

The sloppy efforts by the other platoons did not go unnoticed by the inspection team. Pride showed in Bert's platoon.

The first morning call for each army unit is reveille. In quarters or on a military reservation it's usually broadcast over some public address system. In the field such as at bivouac, one of the NCOs goes to all the tents to roust out the troops. The exact time of reveille will vary little from situation to situation. Reveille on post in a given command will be the same for troops in the field.

A car drove into the bivouac area of Love Company a few minutes after time for reveille and the car stopped. A lieutenant colonel stepped from the right rear door just a fraction of a second ahead of a young second john who hurried from the other rear door.

"I'll find the CO, Sir."

"Stand fast, Lieutenant." The colonel looked around the silent compound. Lieutenant Colonel William F. Elliott was no stranger to the laxity of units not only in the 24th Division but other Eighth Army units as well. A few tents gave the appearance of activity from the shadows cast on the tent walls by the flickering flames from small sterno cans. Most GIs burned sterno in their tent early in the morning to provide light and also take the chill off the tent.

A sound from the trees behind the car caused both officers to turn. A long figure stumbled into the lighter area from among the trees. The soldier shuffled along as he fumbled with his fatigue pants. At sight of the staff car the GI stopped and saluted.

"Good morning, Sirs."

An unseen smile pulled at the corners of the colonel's mouth as he returned the salute.

"Soldier, it's still dark. Weren't you just guessing that there were officers present?" Colonel Elliott asked.

"Oh, no, Sir. If there's a staff car it don't go 'round without officers, Sir."

"I see. Have we missed reveille and breakfast, soldier?" Elliott asked.

"I sure hope not, Sir. I'm hungry."

"No reveille, yet?"

"Oh no, Sir." The young soldier waited at attention a bit uncomfortable knowing that his pants placket was not yet buttoned.

"Carry on, Soldier."

The soldier saluted, turned toward his tent then turned back.

"Did you want me to get the Sergeant, Sir?"

"No, thank you."

The soldier stumbled off into the darkness. The Colonel nodded to the second lieutenant. "Let's survey the camp."

Judging the direction of the distant clatter of pots and pans, the Colonel started toward the field kitchen. His guess was soon confirmed as correct. A whiff of fresh brewed coffee came to his nostrils.

Just outside the area of light from the kitchen, the colonel stopped. A Japanese civilian mess steward busily arranged warm pans and poured scrambled eggs from a large kettle into the pans.

A lone figure in starched fatigues drew a cup of coffee from the large field urn at the end of a distant table.

The colonel proceeded toward the coffee urn. At sight of the officer, the figure at the urn turned and saluted, "Good morning, Colonel Elliott."

"Morning, Sergeant England."

"If the Colonel will excuse me, I'll get Captain Tenley from the troop area, Sir."

The colonel shook his head and selected a cup for his own coffee. "No need, Sergeant, he'll show up."

"Perhaps I can have some eggs and toast brought to the Colonel and his party?"

"No, Sergeant, we had breakfast in the post area."

England saluted, did an about face and carried his coffee into the darkness. Once sure he was out of the circle of light, he disobeyed the colonel's order and played his role in the "Army Game." He scrambled to find and rouse the captain. Captain Tenley was just emerging from his tent as Sergeant England arrived.

"Good morning, Sir." His salute was returned and he continued. "Colonel Elliott is here, Sir."

"Thanks, Sergeant. Roust the troops."

ငશ ငશ ငશ

Later that same day the staff car carried Colonel Elliott and his aide down the winding mountain road to the base. Colonel Elliott broke the silence that endured since they left Love Company's bivouac.

"Lieutenant, you've taken notes and should have all the data you need. I expect a draft report on my desk by 1500 hours tomorrow."

"Yes, Sir."

The car negotiated the curves and switchbacks as the driver orchestrated.

The junior officer suggested his report's summation. "If I may, Sir, it is a shame isn't it?"

"Shame, Lieutenant?"

"Yes, Sir. Failure to hold reveille at the proper time is among my notes." As the young officer referred to his note pad, he continued the litany. "The lack of equipment is pitiful. Second Platoon carrying a log to simulate an HMG. Not to mention the number of men wearing tennis shoes."

"Keep that last phrase in mind, Lieutenant."

"Sir?" A frown sat briefly on the Lieutenant's brow.

"Not to mention."

"I'm not sure I follow. Sir?" The frown on the younger officer's brow intensified.

"First, the question of reveille. That is G-3, Plans and Training territory. We don't do G-3 and they, in turn, don't do Quartermaster inspections for us. The observed shortages may not be the fault of company supply, battalion, regiment, or division. If the equipment is not issued because of its unavailability in Far East Command, the various subordinate units can't be held accountable nor at fault." The Colonel paused a minute then ended, "So don't mention it."

"I understand, I think, Sir. I considered the shortages might best appear in the report to make it a matter of record the lack of complete compliance with the Table Of Organization and Equipment."

"We aren't up to TO&E and the fact is known from your desk to the Pentagon. I want you to review all equipment records to assure us that all red-lined entries are made as appropriate."

"Yes, Sir."

The Lieutenant sat in silent consternation the rest of the trip. If the purpose of the inspection was to assess a unit's readiness, and deficiencies were noted but not reported, would an incorrect assessment be implied? The colonel directed a review of records to make sure all shortages have been duly requested but red-lined as not available. Such a review of the Division records was a tedious and lengthy task. The young lieutenant might have wondered if the assignment was actually a reprimand in disguise?

The Army Game has many forms.

The men spent the first day in the field in dismounted drill marching in small as well as large formations and the afternoon in physical training exercises. The day's routine was conducted by Love Company cadre but all under the watchful eye of the various members of the Division Inspection Team. Two lectures gave the basics of health and personal hygiene in the field. Later in the day the men participated in an exercise in mine laying and mine detection. One last assembly was called after evening chow.

"Tomorrow," Captain Tenley began, "you will be under command of the inspection team personnel. All activities will be directed and evaluated by one or more of the team members."

A brief pause was followed by Captain Tenley's crisp preparatory part of a command, "Company."

The platoon leaders called in unison, "Platoon."

"Attention!"

"Dismissed." The Company Commander watched in silence as the GIs melted into the gathering dark of their individual platoon areas.

The morning call seemed awfully early yet Division was on time. The test personnel routed the three companies of the regiment out in formation and the day began. First activities were camouflage and use of available terrain. Captain Geoletti commanded Bert's platoon.

After exercises on cover and concealment the captain gave the unit a break. The always present search for cigarettes and then matches or lights created a tight cluster of GIs in the demonstration area. Bert, not a smoker, hung on the fringe of the group simply for social needs.

Bert saw Captain Geoletti stroll up near the group in nonchalant fashion. Suddenly something rolled from the captain's hand and into the cluster of men. The captain called, "Grenade!"

The sputtering dummy grenade rolled against a squad member's foot and bounced toward Bert. Quickly, Bert grabbed the grenade and threw it into nearby brush.

The hollow pop of the practice grenade sounded over a mostly prone squad. Bert and others rolled over and sat up.

Caparelli, sat wide-eyed near Bert, "I always thought you were supposed to put your helmet over the damn thing and lay on it."

Captain Geoletti directed them all to stand. As the squad stood, looked sheepishly at one another and dusted themselves off the captain turned to Bert, "Your name?"

"PFC Cronwette, Sir."

"Cronwette, why didn't you cover the grenade with your body like this young man said." The captain waited.

"Well, Sir," Bert felt his face redden as he stammered out his answer, "I's thinking if'n it had been real and I could chunk it away, well, nobody would get hurt. Uh, Sir."

"It could have exploded and blown off your hand or arm." The captain cocked his head at Bert.

"Well. Sir, I reckon, but I's thinking best an arm on the chance of not a kill'n nobody."

"You are correct." Captain Geoletti waved to the entire platoon. "The safety of your unit is the most important thing for you to consider. Remember you are part of a unit. That unit's welfare is your most important concern. The strength and welfare of a unit depends on the strength and welfare of each member of that unit."

The captain turned and walked away. A sergeant from the inspecting team was sent to look for the practice grenade. The break ended in some quiet talk but mostly in silence.

After noon chow, Bert felt better. Embarrassed by the grenade episode he recovered quickly after Lieutenant Perry personally patted him on the back. The platoon was marched to a different area by inspection team cadre. The squads were separated and marched to different areas around a large cleared area. Bert's squad assembled at the base of a small hill and the same captain who had thrown the dummy grenade climbed to the top of the hill. The sergeant sent the closest squad member to report to the captain.

Caparelli called to the sergeant, "What will we do up there?"

"Only what the captain tells you." The inspection team sergeant's terse reply ended Caparelli's questions.

As the first squad member started back down, the sergeant turned and pointed to Bert, "Up to the captain."

At the crest of the hill Bert reported, "PFC Cronwette, Sir." The salute was returned, the Captain made a note on his clipboard, then looked up at Bert.

"In this situation, you're a squad leader. Your squad's mission is to hold this hill in the face of an expected attack. How and where would you place your squad?"

Bert tried to remember their training in squad maneuvers as he looked over the hill. The ridge, some 200 feet long was fronted on both sides by a gentle slope. No geographic features were there. No gully, trees, or opportunities for concealment. Finally confident he had no tricks to worry about, he asked, "What weapons would I have, Sir?"

"What would you like?" The captain smiled.

"Do I know the attacking strength, Sir?" Bert pressed.

"Oh," the captain thought a minute, "let's say an infantry platoon." The captain made another note on his clipboard.

"I'd want two 30s, one at each end of the ridge with fields of fire both front and sides in case of enemy sneaking around."

Bert paused and looked again over the ridge. "I guess, Sir then I'd want the rest of the squad along the ridge with at least two BARs near the center of the line. All units dug in and ammunition supply over the crest of the ridge and available to all except the belts for the BARs. Them I'd split between the guns. Sir."

After another note on his pad the captain looked up, "Anything else?"

"A good communication line or radio to my company command post, Sir."

"Return to your unit, Soldier."

The last day of the field exercises time was spent practicing company maneuvers. Then the following morning the units marched back to the barracks.

⊗ ⊗ ⊗

The Division Commander's Staff Meeting, or briefing, was

scheduled for 1000 hours. As usual an unofficial discussion around the coffee urn and pastry tray preceded the formal conference.

The real purpose of the pre-conference coffee clatch, aside from the obvious, was an informal airing of those items to be included on the agenda. Not necessarily part of what may be called the Army Game, but useful practice in many agencies and companies. Each of the Chiefs of Staff, G-1, Personnel; G-2, Intelligence; G-3, Plans and Training; and G-4 Quartermaster, attended with lower rank support personnel.

The informal discussion prevented any one from being blind-sided in front of the General. Call it SYA, Army Game, or sharing of song sheets, the formal conference proceeded more smoothly after the "coffee clatch." The General concluded the formal meeting with a pep talk and thanked them for their continued effort and good works.

After exchanged pleasantries, the various staff and aides left. The two generals, one Division Commander and the other his Assistant Division Commander (ADC), sat alone finishing their coffee. The older but junior by rank, spoke.

"Sometimes as I listen to these fabrications and half-truths, I worry about a possible disaster. What would our Division do in a real emergency?"

The tall, younger, and sandy-haired commanding general spoke his mind slowly. "Well, the evaluations of the 32d sound encouraging. I guess, however the details of any disaster would determine just how far up the creek we'd be."

Silence sat in the room for only a bit as the commanding general sipped the last of his coffee and continued his thoughts. "We are, in truth poorly equipped and short in every category. A look in our warehouses at dud ammunition and worn out small arms is a daily reminder that the Pentagon will give us only what's left in the budget after they care for Europe. We must, nevertheless, strive to meet HQ's schedule of training and maneuvers."

"I lobbied hard for this assignment as my last before retirement. I only hope it comes before any trouble." the ADC mused.

"My own retirement isn't too long after that." The lanky General stood. "Realism dictates accepting our reports. Every one of us in Eighth Army pads reports, all betting no one calls our bluff in this game."

ℓ ℓ ℓ

"Cronwette!" England's voice cut through the noise in the squad room. The squad's congratulations to Bert on his promotion quieted.

"Here, Sergeant."

"I need to see you." The sergeant disappeared across the hall into his cadre room. Bert followed.

"Sit down, Bert. You now fill a big need in this platoon. I need a squad leader who will listen-up, pay attention, do as told, and give me no grief. You're that man, Corporal."

"It's kinda sudden, Sarge."

"You scored at the top of the platoon in the field exercise. You get those stripes sewed on. Lieutenant Perry was happy with the promotion allocation." Sergeant England shook his head. "Problem is that there can be no pay increase now, maybe after 1 June, beginning of the new fiscal year. The promotion is on the record, for sure."

"Gee, I'm real glad to be promoted, and all." Bert hesitated, blushed and finished. "But I don't know nothing 'bout being a corporal. I can sew on the stripes, then what?"

"I have a plan, Bert." England held up a hand for patience. "Lieutenant Perry and I talked about getting you prepared to be a sharp and ready NCO. I'll be your mentor."

"What is it that you'll do?"

"Teach you what and how to be an NCO." England smiled.

"Like in school?" England didn't catch the edge of fright in Bert's question. In the silence, Bert looked down at his shoes and felt his cheeks flush knowing that he had to confess his reading problem. "Well, they's a thing..."

"I don't plan to ask you to read, Bert." England laid a hand momentarily on Bert's sleeve as he responded to Bert's worry.

"Gosh," Bert looked up. "You know 'bout that? You know 'bout my problem?"

"It's not a problem." England's answer was easy.

"But how'd I help you lead and all?"

England paused a moment then answered. "Let's have a first lesson now, okay?"

"Sure." Bert perked up a bit.

"First, you don't learn about leadership just by reading a book. Now," England paused momentarily, "I want to talk about a unit. We say a squad is a unit, sometimes a section like the mortar section in fourth squad is a unit. Each unit is made up of individuals. The section, squad, platoon, company, say as a unit, is only as strong or weak as the strongest or weakest individual in that unit."

"You mean like last week in the platoon races, Caparelli was the slowest in our squad so we, the squad couldn't run no faster than Caparelli?"

"Exactly." England smiled.

"And like maybe Leggett is fastest, the squad is no faster than Leggett?"

"Right, again." England continued. "You, as the leader of a unit must know the strength of the unit. You must know the individual strengths and abilities. Who's fastest, slowest, strongest, weakest, best shot, and slowest in clearing a hangfire. You, as the leader, plan with that in mind."

"Oh, like is we's going on a march, I'd maybe put Caparelli in front to start?"

"Now you're catching on." England said, "In a combat situation, if you knew two members of your unit were different at clearing a hangfire, one a whiz and the other a fumble-fingers, would you put them in different foxholes or together?"

"Well," Bert paused a minute, then smiled. "If those two was together one could cover for the other like. If they was not together I'd still have to put the fumblefinger with someone to cover in case of that hangfire."

Late that night Bert climbed into his bunk. It was hot in southern Japan that May night but it wasn't the heat that kept Bert from sleeping. He had so many new ideas to learn. He didn't have to read to be a success in the Army.

True to his promise, Sergeant England continued the mentoring. It was not a regular every night affair, but by mid-June, England felt that Bert's training had succeeded. Bert had taken hold of his squad and it was working well. Graduation time for Bert arrived.

After a Saturday inspection and a round of beer at the NCO Club, England turned to Bert, "In honor of your hard work and stripes, I believe we should celebrate by investing in real estate." At Bert's empty return gaze, England explained "Real estate is houses and lots. In this case I suggest we get shut of the base and spend some money on whore houses and lots of sake, Lad."

They rented a pedi-cab from among the group of hopefuls at the main gate and were taxied into town following England's directions to the peddler. John England, among the first wave of Americans ashore in Japan after the surrender, had spent a good bit of time learning Japanese customs, culture, and the language.

One of the reasons Bert had not strayed off-base was his lack of confidence for going in a strange land. In Bert's mind the defeat of the Japanese had only been five years in the past. What if some Japanese still had a grudge and lay in wait to kill any GI they found off-base? With England it was different. He felt at ease when England was around. After all, the sergeant had been in Japan for one three-year tour and was almost finished his second. He not only spoke the language but knew the area well.

Bert found the passing scenery fascinating. Like outside most military bases, even in the United States, a Boom Town had grown up along the road. Here and there a few of the small buildings they passed were actually large military packing crates. One or two even showed stenciled nomenclature on the recycled sides.

The warmth of early summer allowed some crate-businesses to prop open a whole side for business selling cheap trinkets and souvenirs for GIs to buy and send home, or give to their moose. An occasional hut blared music from an unseen speaker. A table or two would be in front with one or two "business girls" sitting and twirling their toes to the strange music. The painted ladies didn't know the GI music but knew GIs thought it sexy if you acted like you knew the music.

Then, as the Boom Town gave way to more permanent establishments, the pedi-cab turned into a side street. This was no store-front business district. These buildings looked more like homes. Each had a board fence facing the street with a gate. No signs, music, chairs, girls, or tables.

The pedi-cab stopped at a small gate. Bert and John England dismounted as John paid the driver. The peddler bowed, England returned a truncated version of the bow and noted for Bert to also bow. They turned to the gate and it opened, revealing a bowing doorman and the inner yard which surprised Bert. Certainly it was not the mill superintendent's yard. No grass like back home.

The Japanese holding the gate open bowed to them, "O hi-o, Engran San."

England repeated the bow and the greeting. Bert did likewise although he had no idea what the name of the state in America had to do with it. The doorman ushered them along a stone path to the front door of the one-story structure. England immediately sat on the small porch and removed his boots. He pulled off the blousing garters and nodded to Bert to do likewise. "Only stocking feet inside, lad."

This presented Bert with new problems. If he left his boots here on the step would they be stolen like happened to some on the troop ship? He decided that England knew what was best. Bert left his boots.

England said they would invest in real estate, houses and lots, whore houses and lots of sake. This looked like a swanky whore house to Bert. The room into which they were ushered was small, plain, and bare of furniture except for two small tables. Small but highly polished, the tables were only two feet tall and the same dimensions in square.

Bert knew what he was supposed to do in a whore house, but he was a bit unsure. Maybe like his old working partner at the Mill would say, Bert felt like an old maid on her wedding night. Something nice was to happen but the details were a mystery.

There were no beds here. Maybe they would go out back

under a big pine tree like Shirley Ann did. But what Japanese woman? He had seen only the little old woman who showed them to this room. He sure didn't want it to be her. He didn't even want to see her without clothes on.

Suddenly his concerns evaporated as two young girls minced into the room, bowed, and knelt across from the already seated Bert and England. England bowed back and Bert followed the lead. The girls each wore the traditional gaily colored kimono, were lightly painted and wore their hair in the Japanese style. England smiled at the two girls and turned to Bert.

"Here's the drill, these two lovelies are the first for us to see. There will be a parade of ladies until we pick two we want. When two are selected we negotiate the price with Moma-san. Once that's settled we'll be with the girls all tonight 'till we leave in the morning. Got it?"

Bert smiled nervously and the two girls smiled in return.

"Gosh, they're both so nice looking."

"Let's see two more?" Without waiting for Bert to respond, England bowed and waved a dismissive hand. All four bowed and the two girls rose and left the room. Bert sat befuddled. It was so open, yet so formal.

A second pair of girls entered, bowed, and knelt.

"Gee, Sarge, how many they got?"

The girl opposite Bert smiled, shyly.

"Hey, I think this is nice." Bert noted aloud thinking of the choice process.

"You sure? You can't change your mind about midnight."

"No, I'm sure." Bert blushed in spite of himself.

England turned back to the girls, bowed and directed, "Mama-san, dozo."

Quickly the old woman returned to the room as the two girls left. Sergeant England and she broke into a quiet discussion in Japanese. At the end of the short discussion, England gave the woman some money and she left.

"The girls will return shortly. You owe me five bucks. Suiko bestows her favors on you for tonight. She's your date." England explained.

Suiko returned, bowed and extended a hand toward the door. Bert bowed, stood and turned to England with a question in his glance.

"It's now 1500 hours," England said. "We'll escort these lovelies to chow-down at 1700 hours. Suiko will know where I am."

Bert followed Suiko down a long hall. Misgivings must have been present in his mind though pleasant. Alone in a strange place. His boots on the steps. Where was this Suiko taking him? Would he get robbed? What if he got knocked out?

Reality. No fear. England said he was a good customer here. He knew what he was doing. Then Suiko stopped, slid a door open, and waved a hand for Bert to enter the small room.

The room was bare except for two small bed rolls and a small box. Bert stepped through the door and waited. He wasn't sure just what, as Sergeant England would have said, was the drill.

Suiko knew the drill. She slid the door closed, unrolled one of the bed rolls, took a plain kimono from the small box, and handed it to Bert. He was puzzled and frowned at Suiko. She pointed to his shirt and pantomimed unbuttoning a shirt. She pointed to the kimono and back to Bert.

He removed his clothes, folded them near the small box, and slipped on the kimono. He was a bit uncomfortable at first, but he had seen grown men on the streets with the same type kimono. It must be okay for men.

Suiko dropped the sash to her kimono and patted the mat. "Dozo?" He looked puzzled and she repeated the Japanese for, please, "Dozo."

He sat on the mat unsure what to do. Suiko, a young but well schooled master of the drill, eased Bert's shoulder down to the mat. She ran a small hand under his kimono and gently stroked his chest then stomach with warm soft fingers. Soon her hand moved down and began a soft massage.

The thrill was great. Butterflies swarmed in his stomach. He also noticed the muscles in his penis began to tighten and swell with the new blood his system pumped in. Wow!

Shirley Ann came to mind. This was no pile of pine needles.

This Suiko was not going to tell him he should marry her.

Suiko noted the arousal she created and smiled, "Quickie?"

His lack of understanding showed in a frown.

She answered with another pidgin phrase. "We fuckie, now?"

ᘓ ᘓ ᘓ

The two GIs retrieved their boots at the front door of the house as the old man rushed to open the gate. He ushered the four to two pedi-cabs at the curb for the short journey. The cabs stopped in front of a two-story building with a paper lantern hanging over the front door. Bert couldn't read the Kanji lettering on the lantern but the outer door opened and the smells announced a restaurant.

They were ushered up a flight of wooden stairs, along a hall, and to a small door near the end of the hall. The host slid the paper-covered door open revealing a small room with two tables and a small kerosene stove. The host bowed and the four entered the room.

A waiter appeared holding a tray with a small ceramic bottle and four ceramic cups, each with a two-ounce capacity. At England's direction the waiter placed the tray in front of England's date, Patti.

She slowly and a bit majestically poured a small amount of the clear liquid into one of the cups and placed it in front of England. She bowed. England bowed and glanced to Bert.

"It is a potent brew of rice wine. Called sake, it's served hot. A few cups will knock you for a row of Sundays. Sip small amounts, slowly."

England bowed in Bert's direction and Patti poured sake in another cup and bowed it towards Bert. He accepted the hot cup and gingerly took a sip. Involuntary tears welled in his eyes as the hot liquid slid down his esophagus.

"Boy, you's right, Sarge. Wow. Hot." He swallowed air to ease the burn of the sake.

"Don't forget, lad. Keep practicing correct English."

"Right. I do forget sometimes." Bert answered then raised a question, "Gee, they sure do a lot of bowing, don't they?"

"It's their custom built on years, even centuries of servitude. They don't understand our idea of freedom. The bow and occasional hiss indicate respect in their culture. In this culture everybody has someone over them. They bow to show their respect and obedience to that person, everyone except the Emperor. They believe him to be divine and not subservient to any mortal."

"It all seems so odd. 'Course I never been to a whore house before. It all seems so easy and open-like. There ain't all that hush-hush like at home."

"In the Orient prostitution is a business. The girls have a contract on them owned by the Mama-san. Mama-san runs the outfit. And don't forget, try not to say ain't. Better to say isn't. Okay?" England sipped his sake.

"Sure, John, I just forget sometimes. But you said something about prostitutes and a contract?"

"In the Orient everyone expects a man to visit prostitutes. He does that to relax."

"You mean like a couple of the guys in our squad have what they call a moose. Is that a contract?"

"Some of our guys do buy a contract. Others go to some of the houses nearer the base, Boom Town. They cuss, fight, get drunk and tear up places. I prefer this type house."

"That 'cause it's quieter?"

"That and because it's a better example of the culture. Besides, these girls," he nodded toward Patti and Suiko, "have done nothing to deserve abuse from us or any other person."

"You say contract. Ain't that like slavery?"

"In the U S, maybe. This is Japan. Here the contract process is legal and accepted." The sergeant sipped his sake.

"Ain't this life kinda hard for the girls?" Bert still lacked full understanding.

"How so?"

"Well, they have to stay there and put up with any guy that pays Momma-san. How'd they get into this?"

England spoke in Japanese to Suiko. She lowered her head a bit then responded in quiet Japanese. When she finished, England bowed slightly and translated to Bert.

"Near the end of the war her father was killed in one of our air raids. Her mother was faced with starvation and sold Suiko's contract for money for the family."

"Sold her own daughter?"

"Yes, a common practice."

"She's owned just like a horse or a car?"

"A hard concept but think for a minute. You and I are in the Army. We have a contract called an enlistment. If next week the Army goes to war and our outfit is ordered into combat, how much choice will either of us have?"

Bert silently pondered what unbeknownst to either was a dramatically prophetic analogy. "Well, I guess not." Bert thought for a minute. "Wow, that's like, worse than living in a mill town."

In the short silence, Patti poured more sake into Bert's small cup.

"But, Sarge, what will these girls do when they get old and wrinkled and nobody will pay Momma-san to fuck them?"

"Unless their contract is bought, they'll be put out on the street to..."

A knock on the door, England responded and the waiter entered with a tray of vegetables, sauces, and slices of both raw meat and fish. England busied himself with preparations. As the sergeant pumped up the pressure on the tank of the small two-burner stove, Bert was lost in thought. It was their way of life and while difficult for him it was not his to worry about. He relaxed into the newfound pleasures of Japan.

It was the beginning of Bert's resolve to stay in the army and enjoy the life it offered. If there was to be a war everybody said it would start in Europe, half a world away. His home was the Army. John England was a good guide, like a father.

Many other young, indulged, over-pampered, soft GIs in Japan shared similar ideas. Across the Sea of Japan events in Korea were fast moving to change their lives. It was Sunday, 25 June 1950.

Chapter 4

"Doin' Like They pays You."

The rumors were the topic of interest in Love Company Mess that Monday night.

"War?"

"Who?"

"Where? Damn, that's close."

"How come?"

"What'd they do?"

"Gooks fighting Gooks?"

The questions were many but the answers few. Few not only for the men in the ranks but also for the various levels of the chain of command. The top levels of command had no priority on the amount of knowledge available.

ೞ   ೞ   ೞ

Orderly Room, Love Company, 32d Regiment, 24th Division.

The officers and NCOs of Love Company crowded into Captain Alvin P. Tenley's office. Many of the questions were those expressed by the other men in the Company. Captain Tenley entered and closed the door behind him.

"Attention!" Called Master Sergeant Brian NMI Barton, Company First Sergeant. Silence followed as all the cadre assumed the position.

"At ease, men." Captain Tenley stood now behind his small desk. As he spoke he laid down a thin manila folder.

"Let me begin by stating that the purpose of this meeting is to enlist your help in laying to rest all rumors about Korea." He paused to be sure he had complete attention to his next statement of the few known facts.

"There is fighting between an invading force from North Korea and the defending army in South Korea. To date the efforts of the Republic of Korea Army to stop the invasion have not been successful."

Captain Tenley carefully surveyed the room, his Executive Officer, four platoon officers, four assistant platoon leaders, and the Company Clerk.

"I want you to clearly understand that what I'm to say here and only what I am to say is a known fact. Any other information from any other source is pure scuttlebutt." He paused, again and waited. With no apparent questions from his cadre, Captain Tenley continued.

"All training will continue as previously scheduled and planned. No change in the activities is to be made at this time. Any questions?"

"Sir?"

"Lieutenant Smithers?"

"The news has announced that President Truman is considering deployment of a unit of American soldiers to Korea. Should consideration be given to alerting those enlisted men known to be living off-base for relocation on-base?"

"A good point and I say not at this time. The prudent course of action is business as usual. You tell some yardbird to stay on base and you merely activate more rumors. We want to reduce rumors." Captain Tenley warned.

"A question, if I may, Sir?"

"About second platoon or supply?" Captain Tenley responded to First Lieutenant Elmer J. Winston, who wore two hats: Second Platoon Leader and Company Quartermaster.

"By initiating the inventory show-down inspection of company equipment previously scheduled for next week would we be flirting with the creation of rumors about pending movement?"

"I think not, Lieutenant. A good point but since the schedule is already posted, it would be more apt to raise questions if we put

62

the show-down off. Business as usual. Do the show-down." After the response, Captain Tenley looked around the assembled staff.

"Any other questions?"

No movement from the cadre.

"Thank you, and remember to keep responses to questions as bland and careful as possible. If you get a situation about which you are not sure, see me." The Love Company Commander ended his speech with one of his almost patented command scowls.

CB CB CB

The steady drone of the C-47 engines had almost lulled Bert to sleep. He was awakened by the tilt of the aircraft as it made a wide sweeping turn. He leaned to the window, straightened up, and looked around just as the Air Force Crew Chief came back from the cockpit area of the plane.

"Can't land your squad, Corporal. The base designated in Korea is rained in. We're headed back to Itasuke."

The Sergeant shrugged both shoulders and walked back through the cockpit door.

"All right for that," grinned Johnston, one of the squad members from his canvas bench seat next to Bert. "My own bed, tonight."

Bert only nodded.

Back on the ground, Sergeant England directed Bert to move his squad from the plane to a nearby empty hanger. Inside, out of the mist that had temporarily replaced the pounding rain, England explained. "The Air Force won't land on a strange field in the rain, with no radar especially if there are no concrete strips to land. We wait."

"Okay, but it's getting late, what about chow or are we going back to our barracks?" Bert queried.

"No transport back to barracks. We stay here tonight. The flyboys are sending over box lunches and coffee. A few other squads from the Task Force will probably be put in here also tonight. We try again in the morning."

Later, after the promised box lunch, which consisted of a dry bologna and cheese sandwich, an apple, and cookie, the squad and the two others quartered in the hanger, had all the coffee they wanted. The morning brought a hot breakfast but more pelting rain.

After noon, the crew chief from the plane Bert's squad had flown in the previous day, came into the hanger and told Bert his squad would be fed then loaded for another try. Sure enough, soon the squad was furnished with another dry box lunch. The flyboys were out of coffee.

This plane flight was uneventful. Even the weather cooperated, to a degree. Just as Bert's squad unloaded in Korea the rain came again with a pounding vengeance, a real gully-washer.

That night the squad huddled close under the freight platform of an abandoned rail depot. Some of the rain was diverted by the loose boards of the platform.

Sleep came slowly to Bert. It was not the steady rain, mosquitoes, stench of nearby rice paddies, but his concern over England's absence that bothered him. Where was the platoon sergeant? Shouldn't even part of a platoon be with the platoon sergeant?

Sure, England had taught him a lot but he had always been there beside Bert in case of a question. Bert had questions. They said at operations the rail depot was in a safe area but should Bert have posted a guard? Who would see that chow was there in the morning? Should they have dug a slit trench?

Maybe England would show up in the morning. That thought allowed sleep.

The next day the sun was out and the squads were loaded onto a train for Taejon. No sign or word from England.

When they left the train in Taejon, a small platoon, consisting of Bert's squad and three others assembled and loaded into trucks. Split from Task Force Smith, the provisional platoon was trucked east to Andong to hold a road junction.

After that disaster, Bert and the four other survivors made their way back to a friendly unit. From there they caught a ride to Teague. The rest at Teague was short and the food catch-as-catch-can. Bert could find not a trace of his duffel bag containing all his clothes.

By 10 July elements of the 25th Division began to arrive in Korea. The fresh division was rushed to the area just north of Teague to help stop the NKPA drive south.

The mauled and decimated 24th Division moved south of Teague to a quieter area of the developing Pusan Perimeter. In that area the division would have a chance to lick its wounds, reorganize, and assimilate replacements.

A fierce drive by the NKPA went down the thinly defended west coast of Korea and made a swing back to the east aimed at Pusan. EUSAK (Eighth United States Army with K now added for Korea), threw together a number of available units to form a provisional company. These worn out survivors were mated to an element of the 187 Rifle Combat Team just arrived from Okinawa by boat. This rag-tag outfit was moved west of Pusan to try to take and hold Hadong.

The Battle to Hadong was only one of a series of efforts by EUSAK to plug leaks in its defensive dike called the Pusan Perimeter. The struggle to hold back the NKPA flood continued to cause terrific problems in the Washington Tokyo Teague hierarchy.

On 14 September MacArthur's landing at Inchon took the pressure off EUSAK.

The 24th Division began its promised rest.

Chapter 5

Old Friends

"Hey, Cronwette!" the Company Clerk called as he passed the tent half.

"What you say?" Bert looked from under a scrub pine where he had tied the canvas. Not a cool spot, yet some help from the September heat of South Korea.

"CO wants you."

The clerk was gone before Bert could question him further. With a sigh, Bert picked up helmet and carbine, and trudged through the mélange of other shelter-halves to the Company Commander's tent.

The tent flap for First Lieutenant Randolph O. Scoggins' command tent was open so Bert waited, half at attention, to be called in. The company commander looked up, and as expected, beckoned Bert in.

"Corporal Cronwette reporting, Sir."

"Lieutenant," Scoggins spoke to the other tent's occupant. The ramrod figure just in front of Bert wore starched fatigues and spit-shined boots. Bert recognized the collar tab as that of a second lieutenant.

"This is your Acting Platoon Sergeant. Cronwette, your new Platoon Leader, Lieutenant Brownie.

"Bert, we meet again."

The new officer turned and smiled at Bert.

"Well, I'll be a, Brownie...ah, I mean, Sir."

"I take it this is not a first meeting?" Lieutenant Scoggins questioned.

"Basic training in the same squad, Sir." Lieutenant Brownie

66

responded.

"Good. Cronwette, show the lieutenant around the area. Let him get his feet in the mud. We'll have cadre meeting 0900 hours tomorrow. New schedules and details from Regiment."

"Yes, Sir." Both saluted, Bert picked up Brownie's duffel and they departed.

Bert and Brownie spent most of the afternoon and night in gaining a handle on the last six months in the lives of the two. Near midnight, Brownie turned the topic to current affairs.

"How do you like the army now that you have to fight?"

"Well, most of the time, it beats hell out of standing on the street corner and swapping pocket knives for a living." Bert shrugged a thin shoulder. "When them damn T-34s are in your area, well that's different."

Brownie picked up the thread of his concern, "How is it that the best damn army in the world is struggling and being pushed into this so-called Pusan Perimeter?"

Bert hesitated a bit before he answered. "I guess it's a question of which army you say is the best."

Brownie looked at his old bunk mate from basic. "You think the NKPA is that good?"

"Well it's kinda like which has the most fleas, the dog or the rug it sleeps on."

"In English."

"It's hard to say whether the NKPA is that good or the US Army is that poor."

"Give me examples."

Bert recounted the failure of arms, ammunition, radios, and artillery at the road junction. He retold the failure of the commander at Hadong. The paucity of leadership and the practice of patching together provisional units and breaking feasible units into smaller units to be fed piece-meal into the NKPA juggernaut.

"Breaking larger units is a problem?"

"Sure, Brownie," Bert answered. "Take for instance my old squad, air-lifted here and sent off with three different squads and called a platoon. We didn't know the other squads or their squad leaders. None of us knew the platoon leaders we had. It's scary enough going into a firefight without going into one not knowing if your leadership can pour piss out'n a boot."

"But you've done okay. Acting platoon sergeant already." Brownie replied.

"Oh," Burt shook his head. "That's just cause the loss rate of NCOs is high and them with combat experience are most rare. It's just being here and having my ass still in one piece. That's all."

A week later, the same lieutenant was cutting through the company bivouac when he came upon Bert stripped down to his skivvies, squatted over a helmet full of soapy water and dabbing at a pair of fatigues. On a nearby scrub pine hung and olive drab undershirt and socks.

"Bert," Brownie stopped at the frail apparition and shook his head. "You've got to get yourself some clothes. Where in hell is your issue?"

"Probably on the back of some sorry-assed Northern slope-head who done choggied north. Haven't seen my duffel since Hadong."

"Take some money to QM and buy a set."

Bert sat back from the helmet of soapy water, and laughed at his friend. "Boy you stateside sharpies got all the answers, don't you? First, I haven't been paid since I left Japan. That's three months. The US can't make up its mind what to pay. Don't want to use greenbacks fear the Commies will glut the market with counterfeits. Won't use Korean Wan cause it's so damn inflated it'd take a duffel full just to spend the night with one o' them local girls. Say they're going to make up a military script. Ain't seen none of it."

"Have you filled out a Request for Survey at QM for your missing issue?"

"There you go, again. Ain't got the OCS starch washed out your pants and figure you know the answers. Hell, Brownie, I done filled out that damn survey thing in triplicate."

"Then you should get new uniforms soon."

"No. Damn thing's come back to me three times. Not enough information, QM said." Bert held up one hand, palm up.

"We gotta get you some clothes." The lieutenant insisted.

"Well, I got the extra pair of skivvies on a moon-light requisition, maybe tonight or tomorrow I'll go hunting again." Bert answered.

"Let me work on it." Brownie shook his head again and walked on.

A week later after a talk with regimental QM, and some of the veteran survivors, Brownie, got both Bert and Carter, also near-naked since Hadong, into a jeep. Just outside Masan, Brownie edged the jeep up to the side of the gate in a barbed wire enclosure. A two-story brick building showing Japanese style details faced the barbed wire gate. Behind that were four GI Quonset huts.

The ROKA Guard at the gate saluted Brownie in an almost rigid position of attention, a trademark of most ROKA soldiers.

"Yes, Sir."

"I need to speak with Sergeant Wong." Brownie returned the salute.

"Ah, yes, Sir. He inside. Must reave jeep, ah, outside."

"Who will watch my jeep from 'slickie-slickie boys'?"

"Yes, Sir. I watch number-one good. Nobody take Jeep." A salute. "No Sir."

The ROKA guard opened the gate for the three Mee-gooks, and saluted again. At the door of the brick building, another guard stood.

"Sergeant Wong, please."

The guard saluted, ran to the first door in the hall, opened it and stood rigid, "Sergeant Wong, inside, Sir."

Inside the large airy room sat an oversized ornate desk, its well oiled immensity dominated the room. It almost dwarfed the smiling Korean behind it. At the front of the desk a nameplate proclaimed in both Han-gook and Mee-gook: Sergeant Wong, Chung Ju, ROKA Supply.

Wong stood and smiled, "Morning, Sirs. How you do?"

"Good morning, Sergeant," Brownie answered. "We need uniforms."

"Ah, have number one khakis for Ruitenant."

"No khaki." Brownie thumbed at Bert and Carter. "Uniforms not for lieutenant, Mee-gook GI can't wear Class A in War Zone."

"Ah, so." Sergeant Wong cocked his head to one side. "Have number one 'Merican made fatigue' for GI." A smile. "Have paper for a-lequisition uniform?"

At a nod from Brownie, Carter sat a canvas bag he had carried upon the counter and unbuckled the top flap. Brownie smiled at Sergeant Wong.

"We couldn't find papers. We looked carefully but found only these. Maybe the ROKA Supply can use these from American supply?"

"Oh?" Sergeant Wong gingerly opened the flap to see inside and then extracted three cartons of cigarettes. "Ah, so. Number one trade." The larcenous sergeant held up two fingers. "We say two sets fatigues each, six pairs short and shirts."

"Boots?" queried Brownie.

"No have boots. Expensive. No have."

"Even the third carton of cigarettes?"

"Solly, no have."

Brownie nodded at Bert and was handed a second canvas bag. As he took the bag, Brownie shook it slightly and watched the ROKA Supply Sergeant's eyes twinkle at the clinking sounds.

"Wait! Chotta Matti. Have number one GI Jump boots. Oh yes, I think you mean other boots." As he looked in the second bag at the two bottles of C & C, the larceny master's eyes opened wider. "Have best, Mee Gook jump-boots."

Riding back to the company compound, Bert mused, "All the trouble the US of A has getting good weapons and ammo over here, I's afraid I'd be naked 'fore we get to the 38th Parallel. And how come them bastards get good number-one GI fatigues and we can't?"

"Our S-4 explained that to boost the Korean economy, the State Department is shipping American-made uniforms to Sygman Rhee at no cost and then buys South Korean-made fatigues from Korean textile mills, for issue to recruits in basic training in the States."

"You mean they give Sygman Rhee and his Forty Thousand Thieves those good uniforms free and let some 'slickie-slickie boy' like that damn sergeant, black-market them?"

"Can't change it, you don't smoke, and you have good fatigues. Let it go."

A week later the 25th Division, now blooded and in full strength moved in just north of the 24th. The 24th was left in what was considered a quiet zone. They were to continue refitting, adjusting to new fillers and collecting overdue supplies but no clothing or pay.

While the Division was in the quieter area, training was ordered for Love Company and each company in the Division's three regiments. Lieutenant Brownie and Bert developed rotational maneuvers. Each day or two the unit would move into no-man's-land on probes and reconnaissance. Each afternoon or after each probe, Brownie called 'skull sessions,' a time to review the patrol, discuss actions, offer suggestions, and generally work at development of the missing element of the first few months of the war, a unit's sense of cohesion.

"Carter."

"Sir?" Carter answered up

"When your squad is moving along a road or route of march keep your eye on the interval between men both in front of you and behind. At proper intervals a mortar round might take out one or maybe two men. Bunched up you could loose a full section."

"Yes, Sir."

"Esteban."

"Sir?"

"Noise. Before any patrol or movement into possible enemy territory, check your squad's gear for rattles. Muffle canteens, keep bayonets away from buckles. If you can hear it, the enemy can too."

"Yes, Sir."

Later the veteran NCOs held informal discussions with the newer NCOs. In combat it's easy for an officer or NCO to be wounded or incapacitated. In order for each individual to understand what should be done in such case, leadership of each unit was often rotated in some exercises.

Bert's ideas always quoted Sergeant England.

"As soon as a patrol or mission is announced set to thinking what your squad will need. What's the worst possible that could happen on the patrol and what would you need. Once you're out there and the NKPA's shooting, no silver supply wagon's gonna come down from above with what you need. Plan ahead."

There were anxious days even after General MacArthur's 'secret' landing at Inchon. The 24th Division struggled to get enough replacements, reorganize, and fill out to its TO&E strength.

Early one morning, having been through the chow line once, Bert stood with his now empty mess kit. "Gonna see if they's any SOS left."

"Is that three trips through the chow line or four?" Lieutenant Brownie mumbled from around a mouthful of his own.

"Best get it while it's here, Sir." Bert responded on his way. "We might have only ice and C-rations tomorrow."

One figure stood ahead of Bert in the chow line. A taller bulky figure, field jacket collar pulled, up and loading his mess kit. He saw master sergeant's stripes on the field jacket sleeve. Bert idled behind him. Then he noticed the familiar stance and movements of the sergeant. A familiar walk. "Sergeant?" Bert asked.

Master Sergeant John England turned in surprise at the voice. "Well, I'll be damned, Cronwette."

The two shook hands as Bert greeted his long-missing friend and mentor. "My Gawd, I thought you'd done bought the farm, Sarge."

An unconscious but reflex action brought England's hand up to his left cheek. Then Bert saw the angry red scar that ran from John's left jawbone almost to the hairline.

"Damn near did." England paused only briefly then pushed on. "You still in our old platoon?"

"What's left of it. I see you got the sixth stripe. Good for you." Bert laughed at his old friend.

"Don't see marks on you. You learn to stay low or just been lucky?" England smiled.

"C'mon over and meet our new platoon leader. A new Second John but a good man."

"Okay, then you fill me in."

After introductions and a second canteen cup of coffee, Bert turned to England, "Where did you get the new face ribbon?"

"Isn't that a beaut?" England's hand tentatively touched the scar.

"I would've thought that'd be a ticket home for you, Sergeant," Lieutenant Brownie commented.

"Well, one thing about the army, Sir, promotions are always available in war. While in the hospital in Tokyo I met up with a friend in G-1, FECOM. He said units were crying for top enlisteds with experience." England thumbed his cheek as he continued, "I have experience." He chuckled briefly at his own joke.

"What about time-in-grade on other sergeants?" Bert questioned.

"I had time-in-grade on Moses at the parting of the Red Sea." England responded in a dour tone.

"You traded this for a ticket home?" Bert was unsure of any logic.

"The last stripe is not always available in peace time or stateside, lad." England commented dourly. "They come dearly."

"What about the guy that sliced you, Sarge?" Bert asked.

"I damn near carried that Kimchee-Popping bastard back to the aid station with me. I had that slope-head skewered on my bayonet like a pig for roasting."

As England paused, Bert prodded, "And?"

"As far as I know he's rotting in some pile of brush near Teague." England turned his attention to his mess kit.

Lieutenant Brownie changed the subject, "What is your assignment, Sergeant?"

"Company First Sergeant, Love."

"Back home. That's great Sarge. 'Slike old times." Bert smiled.

"Yes. Obviously I need to continue your lessons my friend. It is like, not 'slike, jug-head."

Everyone shared in the laughter.

England stood and announced, "I have to get busy. Captain Tenley has officer's call and NCO meeting set for 1030 hours. See you then." Saluted Brownie and was gone.

The platoon leaders and NCOs crowded into the company commander's tent chatted quietly as they waited. Shortly Sergeant England pushed to the front of the tent and called, "Attention!"

Chatter ceased, all strained to the position, and Captain Tenley strode to the front quickly. "At ease, gentlemen." As the captain faced the company's leadership, Sergeant England sat a small table on its edge on a second table and displayed a map. The captain directed the command's attention to the map.

"At 0400 hours tomorrow 24th Division will continue its movement north with an attack up the Waigwan to Taejon road." He pointed to the road on the map as a few sounds of approval came from the men gathered.

The captain continued. "The attack is aimed through this section of road held now by the NKPA. Once through that first narrow pass, the road on into Kumchon flattens out." The company commander pointed to the map.

"Regimental assignments have been made and we're in reserve for this attack."

Tenley raised a hand against the groans.

"Regardless, reveille will be at 0345 hours. Chow will follow immediately and company assembly points designated. We'll be ready at a moment's notice when and if called."

Tenley then summarized the map and its terrain features as well as the planned route of attack and positions of the units in the attack. "Questions?"

An uncomfortable silence pervaded for a minute, 'till Bert raised a tentative hand.

"Sergeant?"

"Well, Sir, I'se, ah were," Bert blushed at his grammatical error but continued. "Just wondering. Them Gooks is real good at diggin' at places like that pass and all. Looks like our attack will be to the front door just where they'll be expecting. I's a bit surprised the attack don't split and hit over them two side-by-side ridges then in the front door when them Gooks is busy with the side attacks. Sir."

"I don't know," Tenley cleared his throat, hesitated then responded, "I'm sure there's a good reason for the plan,

Cronwette."

Tenley looked around, "Any other questions?" Silence followed.

England called "Attention! Dismissed!"

Bert was in the platoon's command post with Lieutenant Brownie when Sergeant England pushed inside that night.

"Welcome, Sergeant." Brownie greeted him. "We just finished weapons prep and about to sip a bit of sour mash. Join us?"

"I'll take that as an order, Sir, but first I want to talk with your tactical expert, here." England waved a thumb at Bert.

"What's up, Sarge?" Bert looked around.

England ignored the question and laid a map on a nearby ammo crate. "Okay, explain your idea for attacking the Kumchon road."

"Well," Bert began, "like any porch-climber knows..."

"Wait." England raised a hand. "I can see I'm behind in your lessons. Tell me in a plain language and not all your crappy country cliches."

"Oh." Bert thought a minute then bent over the map. "The Waigwan/Taejon road goes between these two ridges. That's a mile or half area before the terrain flattens out to Kumchon. The ridges are close enough to the road that our bigger mortars can cover the road from either side. We post our attack infantry and mortar crews on the off-side of those ridges late at night, real quiet like. What I was suggesting was that the mortars take out any big stuff dug in, first light. Then the infantry can attack down the sides of the ridges while them Patton tanks run up the road." Bert looked up and added, "We'd have them Gooks like treed opossums."

England concentrated on the map for a good minute before responding, "We move into the heights before the attack?"

"Sounds solid, Sergeant," Brownie added.

"It'd be nice to look down their throats for a change," Bert mused.

"You know, Lieutenant, with all due respect to the medical corps and its warning against booze while still on penicillin, I'll join you. Just a sip, Sir." England held out a canteen cup. He did not protest till the cup was at least half full of bourbon. With cup in hand England turned to Bert, "Now just what in hell is a porch climber?"

"Hell, Sarge, any old boy knows if you want to go to a party but the front door's locked, you just climb up on the porch and in a winder." Bert shrugged a shoulder.

"It's windoooo, damn it." England held his scowl only a minute then joined the laughter of the other two. England sipped, turned, raised his cup to Brownie and smiled. "Damn good booze, Sir. Always glad to carry out your orders."

"By the way, Sergeant," Bert prodded, "that penicillin you say about, your wound infected or were you keeping company with some of Tokyo's lovelies?"

"Damn Kimchee-Popper. Must have never cleaned his damn bayonet."

The next day all of Love Company experienced a great deal of anxiety. In reserve and at a jumping off point they could hear the battle. They waited. By noon the attack had failed. Six Patton tanks knocked out and the infantry badly routed. The 9th NKPA Division guarding the road was, as Bert had guessed, well dug in.

Love Company, back in their bivouac had lined up for noon chow when Captain Tenley and a lieutenant colonel rode into the area in a jeep driven by Sergeant England. England alighted and called Bert.

Bert set down his mess kit and reported.

"Sergeant, this is Colonel Warden, Regimental S-3, he has questions about your ideas on the Kumchon attack."

"Here," without any preliminaries the colonel spread a map on the hood of the jeep. England nudged Bert forward. "Show me, on this map, what you have in mind."

"Well, Sir, the enemy has a real knack for diggin' in. But now we got them more powerful mortars and H.E.A.T., we could slickie a company with one or two mortar crews, up back of each of these two ridges in the dark real early like." As Bert explained he pointed on the map. "Let the mortars zero in on the big stuff them Goo...Enemy got dug in first, soon as its light. Then let the Pattons come in the front as we infantry comes down from the ridges on each side."

Bert smiled as he finished and added without thinking, "Now I ain't saying that idea hangs up there with the moon, but we'd sure cook 'em, Sir."

The lieutenant colonel studied the map again, carefully as he rubbed his chin in thought. Finally he turned to Bert. "You've studied this map carefully?"

"Well," Bert unconsciously looked down at the toe of his boot rubbing a circle in the dirt, "I 'member how them ridges run, Sir."

"Recon?"

"No, Sir, when I's...I was, a coming south, Sir."

"What?"

"If I may, Sir," Captain Tenly offered, "Sergeant Cronwette was first in with Task Force Smith. I'm sure he remembers this area well."

The colonel and Tenly climbed in the jeep engrossed in deep conversation. England took the chance to growl at Bert. "You don't start telling a damn colonel about hanging a moon, you jack-ass."

With Bert stammering in his wake, England climbed into the jeep and drove out of the area.

At the end of the serving line that evening, each man was given a day's issue of C-rations. An announcement was made that morning chow would be at 03:45 hours. No further announcements need be made. The company began cleaning and checking weapons. Along with morning chow would be issue of ammunition. By dark all were in their sleeping bags or getting ready to get into the bag.

Breakfast consisted of bacon, ham, sausage, along with scrambled (reconstituted from powder) eggs, toast, and coffee. At the end of the serving line each man picked up a carton of C-rations from the stack.

"Brownie," Bert spoke around a mouthful of eggs, "We got two worries. One is noise makers, and possible Gook outposts."

"Captain Tenly has passed the word to all platoon leaders on those scores." Lieutenant Brownie answered. "We're designated point platoon on the east ridge." The lieutenant paused for a swallow of coffee. "I intend to go over the platoon again at the jump-off point. Regiment has scheduled in a few minutes for both that and a careful scout for outposts."

Bert felt different on the ride to the jump-off. There was anxiety of course. It was to be a battle. There was always the possibility of not surviving a battle. Was there fear? No. He was as cautious as ever, but comfortable in the thought that a good plan had been made. The newer heavier weapons gave him confidence. The mortars with the high explosive anti tank rounds should be able to put the self-propelled gun out of action. Yesterday's failed attack at least gave the planners for today the advantage of knowing about the dug-in heavy placement.

Bert also felt good to be working with a well known and trained platoon with experienced squad leaders. Lieutenant Brownie had developed into a smart platoon leader and of course it was always good to have Sergeant England back.

At the jump-off point Bert's feelings were buoyed even more by the banter among the men as they checked each other and albeit nervous, bounced barbs.

"Hey Sergeant, I need some of that R & R soon."

"What's the problem, Rankin?" Bert checked.

"It's Smitty, he's always trying to feel me up."

"Oh shit. In your dreams." Smith shot back.

"Sounds to me like it's Smitty that needs the R & R." Bert smiled as he continued checking the platoon. Toilet tissue sandwiched between canteen cups and canteen; all pack straps carefully coiled to avoid metal tips hitting each other; and pocket items of metal such as church keys from C-rations and knives separated.

The two platoons moved out in dark silence into the unknown of enemy territory.

Bert had scouted the area behind the ridges late yesterday and outlined an approach path for both ridges, and now he was point-man following one of the paths. About half-way up the ridge he encountered the rocks he had noted previously. Carefully negotiating around them he moved the unit along the back side of the ridge always fearful that each of the many copses of stunted pine might hide an outpost ready to give warning to the enemy dug in below the other side of the ridge.

Just short of the crest, Bert signaled the column to halt. A breather was in order. Some GI puffing along the crest like a locomotive would surely bring an alert sentry nosing around.

Soon Bert motioned the column to proceed. All quiet and clear but Bert anxiously eased forward into the dark on the ridge. At last he reached a point he recognized as the spot he identified yesterday as just opposite the heavy gun implacement. With hand-signals he halted the column, eased near the crest, and lay quiet for a minute listening.

He didn't hear a sound. Bert eased noiselessly to the crest of the ridge. He could not see clearly into the bottom of the draw but noticed a point of light or two near the back side of the draw. A small rock was just opposite Bert, its shape in his line of vision. He started to ease past the rock when it moved!

Bert froze. His eyes only inches from the head of an outpost. Bert dared not breathe. Inch by inch Bert slipped down quietly. He felt for his bayonet. With one hand cupped over the bayonet guard and locking mechanism, Bert eased the weapon into his hand. He carefully wiped the sweat from his palm, and gripped the bayonet.

He eased back to his original point just at the crest. He pulled his legs up to bunch under himself, and slowly raised up behind his target.

A quick lunge. He clamped his left hand over the guard's mouth, and as he strained to pull the hapless outpost back to the crest of rocks, ended the quick struggle with two bayonet thrusts; the first thrust to the side of the chest, the second thrust was into the throat to end the possibility of an outcry.

Bert lowered the cooling body back over the crest to its original sitting position just as faint light glimmered over the eastern ridge.

The signal was passed for the advance and soon the three-man mortar crew crept past followed by three ammo carriers laden with HEAT shells for the mortar. Shortly a second parade of lethal promises passed Bert's point.

Lieutenant Brownie eased up to Bert. "Just about time. Are we ready?"

More casually than he felt, Bert drawled, "Reckon."

With a pat on Bert's shoulder, Brownie moved on past followed by another section of GIs. Bert checked his watch. Two minutes. Brownie came back quickly and hunkered down next to Bert. "All set," Brownie whispered. "The orchestra tunes up in less than a minute."

Bert raised up to peer over the crest into the small valley. He could see a dozen or so small fires back toward the Kumchon end of the small valley. The road almost blended in to the dark hill sides. It made a light ribbon cutting between the two hills. Many details were yet hidden from view.

The orchestra tune-up Brownie promised came. The mortar shells dropped into the large tubes gave a soft almost hollow thwump.

"Thwump."

Then a third round was sent on its way.

"Thwump."

Bert strained to see the effectiveness of the HEAT on the self-propelled gun. He could not see, at first. A round from the other ridge struck near the gun emplacement to show the gun barrel canted at a high angle. Half the carriage was gone. Time for the Patton tanks.

The conductor for Brownie's orchestra signaled in the brass section. The tanks entered the valley firing right down the road. The first round from the lead Patton exploded into the mess that had been the self-propelled enemy gun. The follow-on tanks formed an echelon as the valley gave room and tank fire concentrated on the emplacements further in the draw.

A whistle sounded and the infantry charged down into the valley from both ridges. As the remaining North Koreans began to feel the pressure of the tanks and the destruction of the mortars, they began to give way. Soon the GIs had sliced into the remaining small groups of enemy.

The mortars adjusted their fire to put a curtain of deadly explosions at the Kumchon end of the valley. No retreat. Some of the North Koreans tried to climb the slopes and avoid the carnage on the road.

Bert and his platoon launched themselves into the enemy at the road. He busied himself with his bayonet. A North Korean uniform appeared before him. Quick thrust and release. The enemy fell.

Another lunged at Bert with bayonet. Parry, butt stroke to the head, recover, quick thrust, and release. Like the hours of training back in Japan Bert thrust, parried, and thrust again.

No one else in front of him. Bert stopped and looked around. A few GIs chased pursuing North Koreans. He stood breathless beside the road. His thoughts still red with anger and his heart pumping adrenaline. He mentally worked to control himself.

A quiet voice intruded from his side, "Didn't run into any rusty bayonets?"

He whirled to face a smiling John England. The older sergeant stood, rifle in hand.

"Oh," Bert sighed, then smiled at England. "Nope but mine shore needs to be honed and cleaned, now."

"Good job, Sergeant." England patted Bert on the back.

Burt's attention was caught by the burned out hulk of a T-34 tank. He slung his M-1 over his shoulder and walked toward the Russian-made tank.

"Where you going?" Asked England.

"Something I gotta do," he replied.

England watched Bert walk up to the hulk, unbutton his fatigue pants and relieve himself on the hated machinery. As he walked back a thin smile played on Bert's face.

"You okay, now?" a knowing sergeant asked.

"Them things shit all over me and some damn good guys at a road junction. I figured it's the least I could do for them." Bert smiled at the late September sun that just began to peek over the eastern ridge.

CB CB CB

Bert and the other veterans of the early months in Korea realized the difference in the new movement up to and across the

38th Parallel. It was a better kind of war for them. Individual movement included your whole unit. All moved as part of a division in the division's own vehicles. Personal gear and your unit mess traveled with you when they could maintain the pace of the general advance. All enjoyed the feeling of comradship and belonging plus the heady sense of success.

Later October found the 24th Division, now attached as part of I Corps, near the Imjin River. The men awoke to frost most mornings now. Then supply began to lag with beer, cigarettes, and chow not always available where the lead units bivouacked.

"What's new?" was the tired GI's response.

Resistance began to stiffen again just after the Division crossed the Imjin River. After a hard and vicious night without food, low ammunition, and repeated frontal assaults by NKPA, the 24th fell back in an orderly withdrawal. Then they experienced quiet for a few days.

Bert felt better because it was a controlled withdrawal. Artillery stayed with the Division during the move. Rear guards moved carefully. None of the pell-mell flight of July and August.

Bert finished rounds of the new platoon position and in the gathering dark dropped down into the dugout serving as the platoon's CP. He shrugged out of his field jacket and briefly held his hands over the guttering lantern. "It's gettin' a mite cold out there."

Brownie nodded then checked, "All dug in and alert?"

Bert shucked off his boots, squirmed into his sleeping bag for warmth, and munched on a C-ration biscuit. Bert was tired but content. He felt a new self-confidence. He was doing a good job. Again life seemed good. No longer the anxious, nervous, and frightened kid from the mill, he was a battle-wise NCO doing a good job and acknowledged as such by his peers.

ભ ભ ભ

There were some indications that a few of the previous night's attackers were Chinese. A rumor? Maybe. Probably tomorrow would include a probe into the hills to the north. Contact had to be made to keep the enemy on their toes. The new commanding general insisted on maintaining contact. An enemy somewhere was an enemy anywhere and everywhere.

By morning supply had caught up with the division and platoon enjoyed a hot breakfast. The old favorite, SOS, but hot, seconds, and ample hot coffee. The mission that morning was for the platoon to move into no-man's-land. The air was clear, crisp, and a light snow started. They were to move forward until they either ran into resistance or found a more favorable location for that night's bivouac.

Bert followed a small ice crusted stream through a draw. He pushed to look for any tracks in the fresh snow, but was still wary.

A sudden explosion behind Bert shook him. He flung himself to the creek bank. "Mortars!"

Muttering angrily to himself he quickly crabbed backward. Ambush. Luckily the NKPA's forward observer had a bit of buck-fever and called in the rounds before the platoon was in real trouble.

Back to cover, Bert jumped up and sprinted back.

"How able! Haul ass! Back! Back!"

He waved his arm. The squads already started a retrograde. The sound of mortar rounds in the draw became sporadic then ceased.

"Lieutenant," Bert smiled. "I'm gonna get me a spotter. I wanna see if'n he's Gook or Chink."

"Watch yourself, fellah. I'd as soon guess than have to train a new platoon sergeant." Brownie smiled and waved Carter up. "We'll move back a bit more and wait. You give Bert cover."

The two worked up the side of the draw before they moved forward. At a point that covered the entire area, Bert lay prone and studied the sides of the draw. A dark blur appeared, seconds, disappeared near the military crest at the far end.

Bert moved his M-1 to his shoulder and disengaged the safety. He trained the sight on the spot where the dark blob had winked.

The blur appeared again. Bert squeezed off two quick rounds. The blob did not move. He motioned Carter to stay put and slid forward along the draw.

He rolled the observer over. Only one button held the mustard quilted coat closed. He flipped the coat open. A small diamond-shaped patch was roughly sewn to the tunic. He found no other materials or papers. Bert ripped the patch from the tunic, stuffed it in his field jacket, and scuttled back along the ridge. The shelling had stopped. Having made enemy contact, the patrol withdrew. Back in the Division perimeter, Bert took the patch to the company S-2.

Hot chow was on line when Bert got back to the platoon area. He took his mess kit of beans, potatoes, and stew. With a canteen cup of coffee, he hunkered down to eat.

Carter passed by. "What'd S-2 say?"

"Mostly not what they said as what they asked. Had to know all I knew and more."

ဆ ဆ ဆ

The further north from the 38th parallel they moved the more contacts with the enemy they made. Patrols into the surrounding hills found more and more evidence of recent occupation. NKPA or Chinese?

S-2 had been informed by Division that the patch turned in by Bert was evidence of a Chinese Field Army. Everyone became more alert and anxious.

The anxiety was somewhat allayed by the movement of the division in unit strength and within known unit formations. No pell mell provisional groupings as had been at the battles of Hadong and Andong. The movement of the Division was troubling in one aspect: winter clothing issue had not caught up with the front lines, yet.

In late November the 24th Division was placed in line to the left of a ROKA Unit. Bert supervised the digging-in and established fields of fire for the night. At the right end of the platoon's line he checked with the squad dug in next to the South Koreans.

"It's almost dark. Keep a check with the ROKs," Bert reminded Carter, squad leader of the tie-in unit.

"Will do. Any word on the chow wagon?"

"Better get ready for some delicious C-rations, again. Maybe hot chow in the morning," Bert guessed.

"Okay."

"Keep 'em alert. Sleep in shifts. Look out for infiltrators. And keep contact with the Han-gook troops next door. They do tend to get a mite skittish after dark." Bert said.

Back at the CP Bert wriggled inside and held his hands over the guttering lantern for a minute as he reported to Brownie.

"All dug in. Seems quiet enough. Hope, hope, hope."

"Contact with the ROKA?" Brownie questioned.

"Yea, they're as hard to keep calm as a long-tailed cat near a rocker. Most of them were diggin' around in the family rice paddy less than a week ago."

Bert pulled off his boots, sat on his open sleeping bag and pulled the bag over his legs. After munching a few C-ration biscuits, he moved the small pistol from his belt to beside his hip, eased out full-length, and zipped up the bag. He managed to lay one hand reassuringly on the pistol just before he dropped off to sleep. He felt better with the pistol at hand.

In a sleeping bag the pistol was easier to use on a possible enemy intruder than to fumble around unzipping the bag to get at a carbine. He was well asleep when the first sounds of the shepherd's horn shrilled into the chill of the night.

Before he could get his boots on the wail of the horn was answered by a chorus of shrill whistles. Bert jammed the pistol into his belt and ran from the tent as he pulled on his field jacket.

At the perimeter, Brownie scurried from foxhole to foxhole. It appeared calm and quiet at the perimeter.

"What the hell's goin' on, Brownie?"

"From the sound you'd think it was Chinese New Year. It means we're really going to be hit hard," the lieutenant answered.

"They sure like to advertise."

"Division said they hit the First Cav right after a serenade like this." Brownie pointed past Carter's squad's position. "Bert, scoot over and tell our ROK friends to get set, stay calm, and don't get excited."

"That's why the Chinese make that racket. Rattle them ROKs good I'll bet."

Bert scuttled by Carter's position.

"Checking our friends?" Carter called over the noise of the pipes and whistles.

"Yea, they'll be strung up tight as a hog on ice." Bert pointed to Carter as he passed. "Don't forget me, now."

Bert crabbed past the last of Carter's squad and down-slope to get past a large shrub pine. He pushed back up slope to the first ROKA foxhole.

Bert called the password. No counter-sign. He called again.

Suddenly a short shadow materialized in front of him. He saw the rifle swing at his head like a club. As he the rifle arched toward Bert the frightened ROK screamed. "Chinee! Chinee!"

Bert couldn't duck in time. The old M-1, used as a club, hit Bert flat on the side of his head, just below the helmet. The rifle butt sent stars into Bert's head followed by blackness.

The rookie, fresh from the streets of Seoul, ran screaming along the already jittery troops. The flight and screams rolled the entire ROK unit out of their lines and into the night.

When Lieutenant Brownie reported the bug-out, regiment ordered a pivot by Brownie's platoon. Carter's squad and the other two on the line pulled back and formed a wing back from their old position. Bert lay unconscious in no-man's land.

Chapter 6

Into the Camps

The assault waves melted into the dark of the night about 0300 hours. Runners moved from squad lines to the CP (command post) for ammo, food, medics, and orders. Regiment ordered reestablishment of contact with the re-forming ROKA units to stabilize the line. From Lieutenant Brownie to all squads the same message:

"Tell Sergeant Cronwette to get his skinny ass to the CP."

Bert tried to find a way through the dark fog of pain that welcomed him back to consciousness. Severe pain prompted his right hand to explore the right side of his head. His cheek was swollen, sore to touch, but not bloody. The right ear felt sticky. Dried blood flaked onto his fingers but he couldn't see it in the dark.

He eased to a sitting position, moaned involuntarily, and licked his dry lips. He struggled for full awareness, abruptly stung by a sharp pain in his right hip. A slapped hand found not a broken bone but a bayonet at his buttocks.

A growl from behind startled him fully awake. He slowly turned his head to see two forms in the gloom. One of the forms again poked him with the Chinese bayonet.

Corporal Bertram J. Cronwette, Acting Platoon Sergeant was made prisoner of war by the Chinese in North Korea, December 1950.

He was pushed along behind Chinese lines to a bombed out bridge. He huddled there the rest of the night. At daylight he noted that there were a number of other allied soldiers under the bridge. They were held there during the next day. He slept fitfully during the day glad to give his aching head a chance to rest.

A nasty jab from a guard's rifle awakened him near dusk. He stood against the cramp in his legs. Other GIs grumbled as the guards herded them all into a semblance of a line. Bert glanced furtively around the area in the gathering dusk but saw no chance of escape. There was no cover or chance at concealment only a slope of open dry sand down to the dry stream bed. It was getting dark but still too light to hope for shadows to mask any attempt to run.

The guards interrupted his search of the possibilities as they pushed the POWs up onto the rail line right of way to march north. Bert estimated the time close to midnight when the line of march left the railroad tracks. Soon they were herded onto a dark narrow trail that led slowly upward and Bert surmised, along the side of a mountain.

The climb was most telling on the GI ahead of Bert. He frequently stumbled into Bert. Moving up closer Bert asked, "Got problems?"

Through gritted teeth, the GI said, "Bad knee."

Bert eased closer beside the wounded GI to support him. "Let me help."

"No talk," came a harsh warning from a nearby guard.

As best he could on the narrow trail, Bert moved along the other GI's side. The increasing grade of the path made it more and more difficult for Bert. The wounded GI stumbled out of Bert's grasp. Bert stooped to help him up and the prisoner behind them bumped into the two and Bert fell. Another Korean oath came from the guard. Bert scrambled to his feet and caught only a glancing blow from the guard's rifle butt.

"This man's leg is bad. He no walk." Bert explained.

The guard, barely discernable in the dark growled back. "No walk?"

"No walk. Needs help." Bert was relieved that he might be able to help the wounded prisoner. Bert was wrong.

With his bayonet the North Korean guard rolled the groaning GI over the edge of the path. A crackle of brush was heard as the helpless man rolled off the path. A gasp of surprise, a thud, a scream, then silence followed.

Bert was shoved back in line and the column moved on. Bert's mind raged at the inhumanity of the guard. The seriousness of the situation with life or death having no affect on the guard, settled heavily on a stunned Bert.

The column moved along in quiet with Bert lost in the enormity of the recent event. They were all at the mercy of these guards with the compunctions of animals. Almost as if to underscore that thought, a GI ahead of Bert stepped out of line, unbuttoned his fatigue pants, and began to relieve himself. A North Korean guard laughed. A choked cry of surprise then terror followed the GI into the darkness down the mountain. The cry or its echo seemed to bounce in Bert's ear a long time.

Weren't these guards human? No thought of help or empathy for the wounded? No decent understanding of a man's need to relieve himself?

Snow was falling. Bert needed to urinate. There had been no stops in the column's movement. He was able to determine that the mountain rose straight up on the right side as the column drug wearily on. To the left seemed nothing.

Bert relieved himself as he walked. His pants were soon stiff from the freezing temperatures.

Bert had just a thin field jacket to protect himself in the cold. Good protection from mist or light rain, it offered scant help against freezing cold. Food once a day on the march consisted of minimal rations, a thin rice gruel ladled into a canteen cup. Even with a spoon of boiled millet added, the cup was less than half full. The prisoners slept in ditches, under bombed out bridges, and in frozen ditches. Always moved and directed by kicks and bayonets. Bert felt a return of the old feeling of valuelesness he had lived with as a kid.

Without the cognizant realization, Bert slowly reverted to the dirty, frightened, malnourished, and docile child of the mill camp; powerless, cold, worn to the bone, prey to the strong man with the rifle and bayonet.

Winding down out of the deep snow on the mountain side, in the early light of the third day on the march, the weary column struggled into a small village of hooches. As dawn broke on "another beautiful day in the ROK," the POWs were collected in the center of the village.

The North Korean Guards herded the POWs into small groups and pushed them into some of the mud-walled huts. Over the protests of a haggard old woman, a guard pushed Bert and twenty others into one small hovel. Some fell, too fatigued and worn to move aside once fallen. The others crowded in behind.

The old crone still protested to the guard. Obviously the hut owner, she continued to mutter angrily at them. They ignored her. In anger she slammed out of the hut and marched to the officer in charge. Even in his exhaustion, Bert slumped near the outside door, could hear her yammering outside.

The yammering stopped and the officer pushed in through the door. He motioned to a guard and Bert and two other men near the door were moved outside at the point of a bayonet. Once outside, the guard motioned them up the side of the mountain toward a small grove of stunted pines.

Bert's fears instantly grew. To be shot? Left under some damn bush on the side of a frozen damn mountain? Unable to protest, Bert moved through the cold.

The guard motioned at some fallen limbs protruding from the snow. He pantomimed picking up the dead limbs and motioned to the three.

"Stovewood for that damn old crone's hut?" questioned one POW.

Bert picked up a stick. The guard nodded and motioned to the sticks. The three began picking up the wood. Bert noticed a mumbling from one of the POWs and the other two began to move in different directions kicking at the snow as if looking for dead wood as the two slowly spread further apart.

Soon the three were a good five to ten yards apart and moving toward the top of the first ridge of the mountain. The guard hunkered down in the snow and lit a cigarette, probably taken from one of the Americans. The other two continued to fan apart and nearer the top of the ridge. One looked back, noted the guard's lack of interest, and nodded at the other.

90

Both POWs sprinted for the ridge crest. The guard, alerted by the rapidly tramping feet, moved into a kneeling position. He brought the rifle to his shoulder and fired. One POW fell as the second cleared the ridge. The wounded POW determinedly pushed up and scrabbled to the ridge line. The guard's second shot missed. The second POW was gone.

At the guard's first shot, Bert had gone prone in the snow. After the second POW disappeared, the guard muttered at Bert and motioned to the wood with his rifle. Bert began picking up the dropped sticks. Back at the hut Bert was directed to the back of the hovel. The old crone busied herself with the new wood stoking the small fire in the fire pit. The hut's only source of heat, warmed air from the deep pit ventilated out in tunnels slanted up to the centers of each room.

The guard wasn't worried about the escape. One wounded, seemingly a leg, and a good hundred miles from UN lines? The escaped duo were no problem. To Bert's fatigued mind it was obvious the guard had no cause to worry over them.

Late in the afternoon, the POWs were rousted from the various buildings by Chinese guards. The North Korean troops were marching back south over the mountain. The Chinese guards herded the POWs for the last few miles to the Yalu River. The stumbling survivors came into sight of the Yalu, now a frozen ribbon of ice. As he staggered onto the ice, Bert remembered General MacArthur's pronouncement that the troops would "be home for Christmas." It was near to Christmas and Bert shook his head. This was to be his home.

The POWs were herded through the small village of Pyoktong and to a large compound on a nearby hill. Bert was pushed into a small mud-sided hut with a thatched roof. Along with some dozen others he found himself in an already crowded room no larger than nine feet square.

Exhausted, hungry, and shivering from the cold and fatigue, most fell over one another and slipped into a kind of torpor. Bert looked around, saw bare walls, one window that opened into the compound, and the one door through which they had been shoved. The hut's size reminded Bert of home, the mill house where he had grown up with Maw and Paw. He soon succumbed to his body's call for rest and slept fitfully.

The routine called "Brain Washing" by some, began the next day. The new POWs were herded from their huts into the middle of the square compound formed on two sides by the rows of huts for the POWs. A kitchen and storehouse formed a third side. Over a fence, the fourth side, was a barracks for the guards and an assortment of offices and classrooms.

The POWs were formed into ranks in the compound and shivered in the cold. A Chinese Officer strode from one of the guard buildings, through the fence, and mounted a platform in front of the POWs. He stood for a minute looking over the shivering Americans, a few British, and one Canadian.

"We of the Chinese People's Volunteers are here to welcome you to freedom. As the first step toward your new freedom, we will teach you the truth about this war." He paused.

A few of the prisoners looked at one another. The officer's voice was clear, his English good, and his tone adequate, but they found his words questionable.

"Your capitalist government does not tell you the truth about this war. We who are your Communist Brothers will help you learn how the Fat Cats in Wall Street have made running dogs of you and sent you to fight we peace loving Chinese people."

The lecture continued in the same vein for a few minutes 'till one POW hollered, "Go fuck yourself!"

Two guards ran into the formation. One guard hit the protester with the butt of his rifle. The other grabbed the prisoner before he dropped to the ground. The two guards carried the protester to the side of the speaker's platform and began to hit him with rifle butt-strokes, kicks, and then fists.

A grumbled reaction came from the other POWs. They stirred and looked at one another. Before any group reaction, the other guards and a new bevy of guards quickly formed a tight ring of bayonets around the grumblers. Silent but sullen, the POWs now stood still.

"All comrades must know we are here to help you progress to the truth. Once you have learned the truth you will truly be free," the Chinese Officer continued.

The speaker paused and looked over the POWs. As he waited, the two guards dragged the beaten man back to his place in the ranks and dropped him.

"We are not here to harm you. We are civilized people and have rules. You must do as the rules say. If you listen and obey the camp rules we will treat you nice. You will learn. You will progress. All Comrades are peace-loving. If you do not learn, progress, and become peace-loving you will be punished. Do not react against your Chinese Brothers."

The beaten prisoner began to stir where he had been dropped. A moan issued from his bloody face. Someone in the ranks grumbled. The instructor raised a hand. Silence.

"I do not curse you. You do not curse me. We work together to help you learn the true way to peace and happiness. You learn and you will have freedom. You resist and react and you will cause trouble for yourselves."

Later, in the hut, the men discussed the situation and what they had seen.

"We're just prisoners. No crap about learning can change that."

"Maybe we can get more than half a pint of slimy boiled millet if we pretend to go along. You know, pretend."

"Just because they're Chinese, that don't make them stupid."

"Hell, like you never saluted an officer you knew was a miserable son of a bitch? That kind of pretending."

"That's not the point. They'll want more than just listening. They'll want statements and talk in front of others."

"Hell, nobody but those Chinks will believe a bunch of talk in this place."

"Pull your head out, dummy. Remember the UCMJ."

"So?"

"You'd be guilty of violating the Uniform Code of Military Justice. Giving aid and comfort to the enemy."

"Shit!"

A sullen silence accompanied a new reality for most of the huddled GIs. The mass lectures continued but the signs of good treatment did not appear. The half-cup of boiled millet a day continued. No medical help arrived. Teeth began to loosen. Dysentery developed. The worst enemy of survival, a despondent malaise, set in among the POWs.

As the days of hunger, deprivation, and hopelessness grew, Bert reverted to the beaten, hungry, victim he had been as a child. He again felt the hunger he knew as a child. His childhood feeling of being alone in a world with people returned to Bert. He lost interest in his world. Each of the hut's occupants worried and scurried for individual survival.

The Chinese represented the bully on the school playground. In school Bert was always the last one picked for games. At times neither team would let him play. Jock or one of the other mill school bullies pushed Bert around just like the Chinese guards pushed him around in the camp.

Before capture, Bert felt part of a group. He took orders from the leader and gave orders. He was part of the group or part of the chain of command. Here he was nothing but a target for the brutality of the guards and the system. Bert's only possession was his body. His only way to protect his one possession was by giving what the bully wanted. It was not a deliberate and conscious decision but a decision, nevertheless.

ɞ   ɞ   ɞ

"Come in. Sit."

The seated Chinese officer pointed to a chair opposite him at the small table. The Chinese Guard who had led Bert from the hut, nudged him into the chair with a rifle butt.

Bert knew it would be important to look strong and defiant. He tried to sit up and look the way he should. What the trained interrogator saw was fear.

"You are part of the new prisoners in our camp. Because you are new I will tell you how to behave. You behave and you will be treated well."

Bert sat in silence.

"I ask questions you answer."

94

Bert again made no response. The officer angrily repeated, "You understand?"

"Yes." Bert's response saved him from the approached guard's fist.

"Now, what does your father do?"

"He's dead."

"Dayed?" The Officer tried to repeat what to him, from Bert's speech was an unknown word. After a shake of his head the puzzled Officer asked, "What is dayed?"

"Dead. Killed in an accident at the mill."

"He dead. Not dayed."

"How long he dead?"

"Oh, 'bout yar."

Again the puzzled look by the officer, then a smile, "You mean year?"

When Bert nodded, the officer asked, "How come you speak such strange language? Are you American?"

Bert was stumped for only a minute, then answered, "They all call me a hillbilly."

"Hill billy? What is that?"

"I grew up in the back woods."

"You did not go to school?"

Bert straightened a bit as he announced his academic credentials, "I finished grade eight."

Bert wanted to look confident and resolute. He feigned nonchalance and put a hand on the table. The hand trembled. Bert quickly returned the hand to his lap.

"How many years in school?" the officer asked, suspiciously.

"Ten years." Bert responded proudly without realizing immediately the two year difference between finishing grade eight and claiming to have been in school ten years. The officer only watched Bert intently for a few minutes.

Unconsciously Bert's hands were tightening and untightening. The eyes flicked nervously at the guard and back to the officer. The experienced Chinese officer decided that obviously the American was too frightened to try to play a joke.

The officer pulled from a cubby hole beneath the table a pile of clippings and put them on the table. He selected one, a clipping from the U. S. military publications, Stars & Stripes, and placed it before Bert.

"You read, please."

Bert stared at the paper. Printed words. His old enemy. He could feel his face flush. Again forced to try to read. Forced to expose his great weakness.

"Well...Ah...I..."

The officer pointed to the headline of one article. "Read here."

"Amercun GI...Ah...Prl Tran." Bert struggled.

The officer pointed to one word. "What is this word?"

Bert looked at the strange series of lines and curls.

"Ah...Prtd?"

"You do not read well. Here, read this word."

The officer pointed to another headline. Bert stumbled, fretted, and struggled to comprehend as sweat popped out on his forehead. The ds and bs, ps qs and gs were, to Bert indistinguishable. Finally Bert hung his head in defeat.

"I don't read so good."

The officer sat silent for a while then nodded at the Guard. Bert was prodded out of the warm office, across the cold compound and into the freezing hut crowded with other shivering GIs. Bert picked his way to his corner. He sank to the little open space and curled into a fetal position.

Shamed. A failure at school. Patsy for a girl wanting his paycheck. A failure in a damned Chinese POW camp. He couldn't even look good before the enemy.

Chapter 7

A Plan

Four Officers of the Peoples Volunteer Army sat around the glowing brazier. Comfortable from the winter winds that howled around Camp 5, they nevertheless cradled the small ceramic cups of hot tea for its extra warmth to their hands.

The four members of the army's special program for the education of prisoners had worked as a team for years re-educating captives from the Nationalist Army and suborning many of those to join the Peoples Army. Although well accustomed to each other, they maintained the expected formality. The Senior Officer, Comrade Leader Chi, spoke slowly.

"As we know it is our task to carefully consider each of the new prisoners. We will separate the weak from the strong."

He paused, leisurely sipped from his ceramic mug, sighed contently, then continued. "The plan is as we practiced in our homeland. We dealt well with the Nationalist Devils. Those here we find to be weak of purpose and who lack understanding we must mark for special help. You have began this part of your work admirably. Always keep your four steps to new understanding in front of you as enumerated by our Beloved Leader."

As he held up his hand and began to recite the plan he consecutively pulled down a finger.

"First, determine the weakness. Second, explore that weakness. Third, make your plan to use the identified weakness. Fourth, work that plan." He paused to look at each of the three subordinates of the Special Corps for Peoples Education. One officer, Bert's interviewer, spoke.

"Comrade Leader Chi, is it possible to obtain a special book? I have one among those new ones one who according to step one, is weak and may present an opportunity for our work. The book will guide me through steps three and four of our venerable plan."

"Give me the name of the book and I will send for it." The Comrade Leader sipped from his mug, and continued. "Is this one who may believe our philosophy?"

"This one, a frail corporal, does not display enough wisdom to have a philosophy. He does show signs of a disability. If it is as I suspect, the book I seek will not only verify my suspicion but help me devise a plan to use his disability." The explanation completed, the younger officer bowed his head slightly to his comrade leader.

"There is a name for this soldier's disability, Comrade?"

"A suspected disability, Comrade Leader."

"Continue, please. What is the suspected disability?" The last may have contained a bit of sarcasm.

"While a student in one of the American Universities, supported by Our Great Mao, I was a student assistant at a reading clinic. The work was with a disability that kept a person from being able to understand the meaning of some symbols used in written English. The disability is called dyslexia. I would explore this possibility, Comrade Leader."

"A disability of the eyes, then, Comrade?"

"Forgive me for not explaining further, Comrade Leader. The problem is in the brain and the connections of the neurons. I believe it is a disability not known by the soldier."

ଔ   ଔ   ଔ

The first days of privation, disease, and stringent controls that was so foreign to the GIs had now become routine for them. With the passing of the winter days the Manchurian winds allowed an occasional warmth to make it almost comfortable were it not for the crowded conditions, poor diet, and imprisonment. Breezes along the Yalu River Valley were occasionally almost balmy. Vegetation that had been stark and barren in winter, showed a few leaves, stunted and scrub, but green.

The ice that had been a constant crust over the thatched roofs began to melt. Constant drips from the melted ice into the huddled POWs was only one more additional discomfort. Nights were still cold, but on many days the field jacket, worn and threadbare at best effected some warmth.

On such a day in Spring of 1952, Bert was called from the hut by a guard. He was glad to be called out. He didn't want to be part of the discussing, plotting, and scheming about a POW Olympics that was current in the hut.

"Look, if the Chinks want to stage a POW Olympics, let them."

"A Summer Games?"

"Why would we participate for them?"

"Yeah. They're sure to make big press of it."

"They'll have to feed us better."

"Hell, they'll only say our activities prove we enjoy life in Chinese Camps."

"So? With the exercise they'll give us more food, and any activity beats hell out'a sitting in this cramped and smelly hut day and night picking nits."

In the interrogation room, Bert sat opposite the officer who had interrogated him last winter. The officer pointed to a tray of rice cakes.

"You would like a cake? I have tea for you." The Chinese poured a small ceramic cup full of a hot tea. The cakes smelled good. The ceramic cup reminded Bert of the sake he had shared with Sergeant England. That seemed eons in the past.

"Help self," insisted the officer.

Bert chewed a tentative bite. It seemed all right. He quickly finished the cake and took a sip from the cup of steaming tea.

"Comrade, I have thought carefully of your reading problem. I want to help you learn to read."

Bert sat silently. The same promise. Each time made, each time broken. The army's promise was most hurtful. Promised by the Recruiting Sergeant he still couldn't read.

"You want to learn to read, Comrade?" The officer smiled at Bert.

"I'm sorry, Sir. They's lots of folks say they's going to teach me to read. It don't happen."

"I have books on reading." As the officer spoke he waved a hand in the direction of a small table in the corner where five or six books lay stacked.

"You may have problem with eye nerves that connect with the brain. New research at University of Michigan reports way to learn to read. I will do some tests. Will you work hard to read?"

"I'll work," Bert's interest peaked. "May not help."

"We see, Comrade."

Bert reached for another rice cake. The officer moved the plate away.

"We study now. Eat later." Then the Chinese gave Bert a list of words. "Draw a circle around each word you do not recognize."

Bert did that and a second list was given him with the same instructions. A third list. A fourth. One list was all words that were easy to recognize. Two lists were all hard.

After the tests Bert was given another rice cake, a cup of tea, then sent back to his hut. Both were happy. Bert felt good because he knew almost all of the words on two lists. The officer was happy. His plan may work.

That night Bert ate his regular cup of fish soup, rice, and millet. In all the diet was not too difficult on Bert. He recalled going to bed when young after only some boiled greens and a spoon of mush. He remembered sometimes at home there had been nothing to eat.

ߛ ߛ ߛ

The four education officers sat around a small table in the open area behind their usual meeting and interrogation room. The Comrade Leader had led a discussion of the Third of Chairman Mao's Rules. He lifted his cup and smiled.

"Tell me how your work with the American who has a reading disability is progressing, Comrade."

"The book that you were so helpful to obtain has given me good insights into this disability. I am now ready to put my plan into execution, Comrade Leader."

"Ah, yes." Comrade Chi smiled. "Please outline your plan for our enlightenment."

"There are certain words in the English language with letters the American's disability doesn't let him identify. When I remove those words from our lecture script or exchange different words that do not have the offending letters, he reads them well. He is intelligent enough that he can remember the information."

"That is all well, Comrade." Comrade Chi smiled tightly. "How does it help our goals."

"He is ashamed of his lack of ability. He is anxious to prove he has learned to read. He will answer questions in the lecture."

"You do well with this one, Comrade." The comrade leader's eyes brightened as he sipped his tea.

ೞ ೞ ೞ

The POWs were herded into the lecture room and pushed into sitting positions on the bare floor. They were thankful it was no longer winter. Then the floors were like ice. The officer who worked with Bert on his reading came to the stand in front and started talking about capitalists. The Chinese officer talked about people who get rich and have money. These rich ones have others fight wars of aggression.

Bert listened carefully. That was what they had read about just before the class. He remembered reading about rich paying others to fight in war. Boy! He read correctly. He wished Old Jock or Betty were here he could prove he was no dummy. He listened carefully to the officer.

"Now, Comrades you have copies of our study for today. I know that some of you were not taught to read well by the capitalist fat cats in America. The other education officers and I have worked with some of you to teach you to read. I would like one of those who has learned to read to tell us what he learned from the study material. Will one of you who can prove he now can read answer a question?"

Silence. The officer now looked at Bert.

"How do the fat cats in America get their money? How?"

Bert stuck up his hand, a bit unsure at first, then straight up.

"Yes, Comrade. How do fat cats get money?"

"They...uh...take it from workers."

"Excellent. We now know that fat cats take money from the poor workers like you. The rich people exploit all workers. They pay them low wages, then take the money back in high taxes. This Comrade can read. He knows about the capitalists. He has read the truth."

Bert felt good. Now everybody knew he could read. His teacher at the mill school would be glad to know this.

After the lesson, as usual, the POWs were herded back into their huts and a Chinese monitor came in to lead a discussion of the lecture.

Master Sergeant Pate, the POW beaten the first day in the camp, hollered at Bert. "Cronwette, you keep your mouth shut."

"I didn't say nothing."

"You got up like some Sunday School kid and spouted off that damn Commie Crap."

"I didn't say nothing bad, I's just proving I can read."

"I don't care if you can read, keep your mouth shut, dammit."

The Chinese hut monitor waved a finger at Sergeant Pace. "You must let him talk. He is learning to read. He is progressing. You must all become progressive. You must learn to cooperate. If you do not work with your Comrades, if you are reactionary, you will be punished."

The monitor scowled at the others. "Now, sit. We talk about lesson."

That night Bert's food cup contained a piece of pork. None of the other cups Bert saw had any meat. Bert ate in silence. He was trying to puzzle out the day's events. He had wanted to read almost all his life. Now he was learning to read. The officer let him speak to prove he could read. Bert couldn't understand why that was so wrong.

ଔ   ଔ   ଔ

Another discussion about the morning's lecture took place.

This at a table in the warm open area in back of the Education Officer's office.

"I see that your plan seems to work doesn't it, comrade?"

"I am honored, Comrade Leader, but also troubled."

Comrade Leader Chi only cocked his head to one side and waited, politely.

"The hut monitor reports that my student was warned not to talk in class."

"That is bad."

"I request that the reactionary American sergeant be moved from that hut, Comrade Leader. If the hillbilly American is not threatened, he may continue to progress."

"I will see to it, Comrade."

੪ ੪ ੪

The process was set as the Chinese officer's routine in his efforts to dupe Bert. The next lesson for Bert was just before the lecture for the entire compound's POW population. The material prepared for Bert to study was carefully re-written to eliminate all of the consonants difficult for Bert to decipher. Bert practiced reading just before the material was presented to the POWs. Bert was asked a question. Poor Bert knew the answer. He could read.

Bert was eager to answer questions about what he had read. He knew about "Fat Cats", "Rich Blood Suckers", unfair labor practices in mills and mines, and the high interest rate charged by bankers. For the first time in his life he could read. More important to Bert, he could prove that he could read.

After the evening meal of rice gruel, Bert sat in his corner. He enjoyed the extra piece of pork and the crust of bread in his cup. Unfortunately, Sergeant Pate had not been the only reactionary in the hut with Bert. That evening one of the other reactionaries made his way across the hut to Bert.

"So you got your Comrades to move Sergeant Pate, huh?"

"What you say?" Bert looked up, not understanding the accusation.

"You talk too damn much. Matter of fact I'm changing your

103

first name to Birdie. We don't want to hear a Birdie sing no more."

"I'm just learning to read. It don't hurt."

"Oh? Let me show you hurt."

The reactionary hit Bert hard. Bert fell back into a corner from the blow.

"Now you damn hillbilly, you help those damn Chinks again and it'll hurt worse."

Bert stayed in the corner slumped where he had fallen. Through guarding fingers he watched the attacker make his way back across the hut to his place.

Bert was confused. Through ten years of struggle in school he had wanted to be able to answer questions in class. Just once it would have been nice to have the teacher smile and say he had done good. Now he was able to answer the questions. By answering the questions he proved he could read. Yet these guys didn't want him to prove he could read.

That night he dreamed he was back in the mill school in his ragged and torn uniform. His teacher stood at the front of the class. She asked him to read from a list of words. He read them all correctly. She called him to the front of the room. When he got up in front he saw the teacher was wearing a Chinese officer's uniform. Astonished, Bert turned back toward his seat. All the students in the class were either Shirley or the mill school bully, Jock. They all laughed at Bert just like they had always done.

The next morning a tired and confused Bert came back from latrine call. As he picked his way back to his place he noted a different person next to his spot. Bert sat down and the new person eased toward Bert and said softly, "Hit you a good 'un last night, didn't he?"

Bert looked closely at the speaker. The other smiled slyly through a scraggly mat of beard and hair pulled forward over his face. He sat quietly. He had not pulled away from Bert's corner as some of the others had this morning.

Bert eased a tentative finger to the side of the face and poked warily at the cheek bone. "It's all right." Bert mumbled.

"I figured when you started to answer questions in class you's gonna get it."

"How come it is they don't want me to learn to read?"

"They don't care why you talk. They just don't want nobody to talk in class or answer questions."

Bert continued to massage his cheekbone with his finger. Recollection. "I know you. You's on the troop ship."

"That's right. KP on that fat-ass'd sergeant's mess deck."

"Todd. I 'member, now. You's in a plane before me. How long you been here?"

"Long 'nuff to know they's ways to ease life a mite." With that Todd pulled his knees up, wrapped his arms around them, and put his head down.

When they got their cup of boiled millet Bert explored his piece of pork quietly. Todd leaned a bit closer, "See you got your extra bit of meat."

Bert wasn't sure how to answer.

Todd shrugged a shoulder. "It's okay. I get's extra meat, all the time."

Bert sat for a minute then asked quietly, "How come?"

"I's friendly with them Chineemens."

Bert studied the mat of hair with shifty eyes peering out from under then responded, "I's just learning to read."

"And I's just doing what I can to get along." Todd shrugged

For the next few days the pain of the cheekbone was replaced by frustration. It had felt so good to be able to answer questions and prove he had learned to read. How was it so bad?

He didn't talk with Todd for a few days. As a matter of fact, Bert was not sure he wanted to talk with Todd. He wondered why Todd got extra meat.

Bert's next lesson did not go well.

"I ain't so sure you're just a teaching me to read," Bert accused.

"You know the words now, don't you?" was the answer.

"Yea, but them other guys say what you teach me to read is not good to say."

"You have to decide." The officer shrugged.

"It ain't easy to decide that."

The officer motioned to the guard.

"Our pupil does not want to read. He comes here with a bruise on one side of his face. We should make the other side bruised."

With a half-swing the guard's rifle butt hit Bert's face. Bert sat stunned on the floor where the butt-stroke left him. His first reaction was anger. He struggled to hold it in. He was helpless.

"Go back to your hut and think. Shall I have the guard help you decide about learning to read?" The Chinese officer glared at Bert. "First maybe you think about learning to read. I will ask again, later."

Bert faced a beating regardless of what he did. If he talked in class he'd be beaten by those called reactionaries because they reacted to the Chinese rather than learn from them. If he didn't talk, the officer would have the guard beat him.

Without explanation Bert's next lesson was cancelled by the Chinese. That night after their gruel, Todd sidled up and sat down by Bert. "I see you ain't got no extra meat for a couple o' days."

"I ain't sure they is teaching me to read."

"What?"

"That officer give me stories to read. I read and understand them. In the compound lecture he asks questions about what I read. Maybe he just teaches me so I'll know what he wants to have me talk about."

"Why sure. They want you to talk in class. If you do then you get extra food."

Bert sat for a minute. If he answered questions that was a favor to the Chinese they were willing to give him extra food for the favor. He turned to Todd. "How come you get extra? What favor do you do?"

The other smiled slyly. "Just cause I's friendly. 'Cause I help them Chineemens."

"How are you friendly?"

Todd only shrugged a shoulder. "You be friendly to them, like answering those questions in class, you'n me is friends." He paused significantly. "You don't then we ain't."

He pulled up his knees, wrapped them in his arms, and put his head down.

The winter of 1952-53 was worst for Bert. One time he answered an innocuous question. As a reward by the hopeful Chinese officer, Bert was given a new blanket. It was taken the first night. He was also beaten by one of the reactionary POWs.

Bert became the acknowledged patsy for all POW problems. Every plan or discussion that took place in the hut became known to the guards. Bert was warned or beaten because of the information leak. The POWs surmised that Birdie Cronwette was the hut's snitch.

Bert never asked but always wondered why nobody ever asked about Todd's extra meat. The Chinese officer never bothered to bring Bert in for lessons again. Once in the compound, the officer stopped Bert.

"You not help Comrades. Comrades will not help you." The officer snarled.

Bert tried again to find out about Todd. He realized that the cold and hunger were common problems for all the POWs, but Bert noticed that neither hunger nor cold bothered Todd.

One night after the routine cup half full of boiled and slimy millet, Bert leaned closer to Todd. "You ain't bothered so much by all this cold. How come?"

Todd snickered and whispered, "That's 'cause I got friends as helps keep me warm."

"What you say?" Bert asked suspiciously.

"Hell, like I been telling you, be friendly to them Chineemen and they'll be friendly back." As he spoke quietly, Todd slyly raised the bottom of his filthy fatigue jacket to reveal olive drab woolen long johns.

Bert's mouth dropped open at the sight of the heavy winter underwear. He stammered then whispered, "Who give you that?"

"I keeps saying to be friendly with them Chineemens." Todd smiled unseen in the dark cold hut.

"But, but you can read and, well you don't say nothing in class."

"Hell, I been friendly with them since I got here." He nudged

Bert with an elbow, "I talk lots."

"But what do you know and talk to them about?" Bert frowned even though Todd could not see him.

"Gawd," Todd gasped. "Just how high up the mountain was you when you fell on your head? It ain't what I know, it's what I hear that them Chineemens like to know."

Bert sat in silence and pondered briefly before he realized Todd's scheme. "Then you saying," Bert's whisper was slow and quiet, "you tell them what these other guys plan and say?"

"I get's fed and extra warm undies."

"But they's on our side?" Bert protested.

"Yea? What'd they ever do for me?"

Bert was astounded, "They's in the same army, same one as you."

"Humph! Like that damn corporal whose chops I busted in basic? He was in the same damn army. I still got six months in the cross-bar hotel for that. They done tacked six more months on my enlistment and made me go through all of basic again. Then that fat-ass'd mess sergeant, they's in the same army. Well, fuck the same army."

Bert pointed at Todd, "Don't know 'bout that corporal, and I ken figure that mess sergeant and all," Bert spread his arms to encompass the hut of sleeping POWs. "But these guys? These guys ain't done nothing to you."

"Same damn army." With that explanation that to Bert was no explanation, Todd ended the conversation in his usual way. He pulled up his knees, wrapped his arms around them and put his head down.

As spring 1953 began to awaken the miserable stunted vegetation in the Valley, the consensus was there. Bert was a progressive. Commmie Cronwette. Birdie. Camp Snitch.

As spring ran to early summer, attention shifted away from Bert. One evening he sat down with his cup of food. There was no gruel of slimy boiled millet. Instead his cup contained a piece of pork, half a slice of bread, and some boiled greens. He was nervous at the discovery. He had done nothing. Were the reactionaries going to beat him some more?

He looked around carefully. Every cup had extra bread and meat. What was going on? The other POWs were confused also.

"What're they up to?"

"Eat quick, it may be a mistake."

"Is it May Day?"

The extra food that night was not a mistake. The next morning the POWs were given a breakfast cup of hot oatmeal. A slow change was made in the diet at the camps. Rations increased. Basic medical care became evident. A Chinese doctor came around to do a quick examination of each POW. On sunny days the POWs were moved outside into the sun. New clothes were issued and there were no more lectures.

Late one night in early August, Todd eased next to Bert. All the other POWs were asleep.

"Psst. How you like the better chow?"

Skeptical, Bert only grunted.

"Liken I say, could be a lot better if you's friendly to them Chineemen."

"We ain't got no more classes."

Todd surveyed the sleeping POWs carefully, leaned closer to Bert. "How'd you like to go to Chinee?"

"What you say?" Bert peered at the mat of hair Todd still wore in front of his face.

"You be more friendly you could still go to Chinee. No more crap from the Army." Todd punched Bert with an elbow. "And they got women in Chinee."

"What you say?"

"Just think about this. The ol' U. S. of A.'s about to sign a agreement thing with Chinee. They's agreed that any POW as don't want to go home don't have to."

"Not go home?" Bert was stunned.

"Better think. You and me go home that army's gonna break bad on us. All these guys is gonna say we was too friendly with them Chineemen. If we go to Chinee we'll be heroes. We can live free, have good food, and all the women we want. 'Sides, won't have to put up with the likes of big-mouthed corporals or that fat-assed mess sergeant."

Bert sat frowning.

Todd leaned closer and whispered. "You just think. All these bastards that beat on you is going to say you and me collaborated. Hell, we'll probably get court martialed. Going to China is free. Think about it."

Todd moved away and left a sleepless and worried Bert.

The next morning as they were being pushed outside to exercise, Todd was close to Bert.

"Look. To go to Chinee just watch me. When I walk away you just follow. We'll go to Chinee with some o' my buddies."

Todd was gone. Bert kept an eye on him as they were pushed in a walking circle around the compound. It was a sparkling spring day in the Yalu Valley that morning but it was a harsh winter in Bert's troubled mind.

Court martial? Why? For proving he had learned to read. Why shouldn't the army be glad he could read? But, go to China? He didn't know anybody in China except Todd, not an encouraging thought. There just wasn't any reason to go to China. He didn't believe there would be any court martial. He would go home.

Prodded by the guards, the POWs continued to move in a circle. Todd edged to the outside of the circle. As they walked to exercise, Todd turned to Bert, smiled, and inclined his head in the outer direction. Todd stepped to a door in the fence by the interrogation hut, it opened, Todd was gone. Bert shook his head and kept moving with the POWs. The Chinese had tricked him once. Not again.

That night, after another full cup of meat, bread, greens, and a separate cup of coffee, Bert got his first real hint of what Todd meant about the army getting down on Bert. One of the reactionaries made his way across the hut to Bert.

"How come you didn't go with your Comrades, Stoolie Birdie?"

"What you say?" Bert was unsure.

"Comrade Todd is in a special hut with his other collaborating buddies. Isn't that where you belong, Comrade Birdie?"

"I ain't no damn comrade."

The other POW glared, "That'll be for a court martial to

decide, Comrade."

In late August the Armistice agreement was signed and preparations were made to leave the camps.

"Going home."

"Now you pay, you sniveling Commie."

"Your time is coming at last, Comrade Birdie."

Bert received no more beatings. At last the POWs were herded into trucks and busses for the long ride to Panmunjohn. Now, on the ride south, in place of beatings warnings were snarled at Bert. The other POWs shunned him. He felt isolated. He was crowded away from on the truck, the bus to Panmunjohn, and at the Freedom Gate. At the 21st Evacuation Hospital where a careful physical was given the individual POW, the threats continued on the sly. In the interest of self-preservation, Bert tried to stay close to officers, medics, and MPs.

Chapter 8

On the Boat

Bert remained worried, watchful, and alert. In his heart he had done no wrong and hadn't harmed anyone. Disappointed that this was not a shared idea, he took the snarled warnings to heart. At the Freedom Gate Ceremony, there was no denouncement or accusation. As he left the Chinese bus and walked under the archway, he was greeted by a burly marine sergeant who shook Bert's hand and bellowed a big "Welcome home, Son," just as he greeted all the repatriates.

Some had worried that the circumstances of capture would somehow stain the POWs in the eyes of the welcoming committee. Far from the case, great joy and happiness greeted the repatriates, one and all.

Photographers and reporters thronged around the processing POWs as they were organized, loaded onto busses, and transported to the 21st Evacuation Hospital for a complete medical evaluation.

Two days later Bert's anxieties crept back into his awareness. Two different times, once as they gathered at the hospital for the ride to the Port of Inchon, and again at the pier, Bert saw a small group of POWs standing to one side intent on a discussion. At times one or the other of the group would look at Bert. Could they be plotting about him? He must remain watchful.

Why didn't they understand he was just learning to read? A skill he was sure all of them had retained since early childhood had been denied him. What was wrong with wanting to prove that he now was able to read?

Once aboard the ship that was to carry him and the others home, Bert began to relax and enjoy himself. The repatriates were gathered in the large mess hall. Before any food was served, a set of three officers walked to the front of the room. A tall one stepped forward and raised both hands and waited for quiet. "Men, on behalf of myself and the other two chaplains here representing the major faiths, welcome to the next step in your journey back to home and loved ones."

A few shouts of joy and a round of applause sounded.

The Chaplain raised a hand for quiet then turned to one of the other two. "Rabbi Baum will lead us in a short prayer of welcome."

The rabbi's prayer sought peace in hearts, forgiveness for all past trespasses, and after the prayer the three chaplains announced their availability and locations for services and individual talks with any who wished.

The ample dinner that night consisted of salads, flavored gelatin, well-strained hamburgers with all the onions, lettuce, and tomatoes, milk in quantity as well as coffee. A few special dietary needs were catered based on the medical staff's references.

Bert felt good. His best day yet, he thought. Good meal, on his way home, and safe on the ship. He was not particularly religious, yet the prayers by the chaplains helped the feeling of well-being. He hoped the good feelings were shared by all, particularly the forgive and forget parts.

Bert decided to take a walk on deck in the evening hour. The sun was setting just astern of the ship and the breeze was cool. As he walked he remembered his first trip on a troop ship so many years ago. A lifetime away it seemed. He remembered the first two years after that first trip as interesting years. The memories of Andong and Hadong, he felt were outweighed by the good of encounters like Kumsong and the feeling of comradeship he had enjoyed in the units and the moves above the 38th parallel.

He was feeling stronger now. His health seemed good. The doctors were impressed that he had not suffered the severe debilitation of so many of the others who were not used to a minimal diet as Bert. Now he was faced with the question of what to do now. Technically his enlistment was up a year or more past. Should he reenlist? Surely the foul-up over his promotion to sergeant would be cleared soon. The army had been a good life. At least one thing he knew, he would not go to work in any damn dirty and noisy mill.

He noticed in the collected darkness the green ocean had turned to a deep blue, almost black. One more turn around the deck then maybe down to the dayroom set up for them. Maybe there was a movie to see. That would sure be a nice thing.

He had just passed a passage way and noticed from the corner of his eye some dark shadows approaching. He paused to let them pass but instead he was seized from behind. A man grabbed each of Bert's arms. A rope passed briefly over his head and his arms were quickly tied to his side.

"Hey!" Bert yelped, startled.

The protest died quickly as a gag was stuffed in his mouth, a cloth secured behind his neck held it in place.

"Mumpff!" He tried again to protest. The faces he saw before him bore snarls of hatred.

"Corporal Cronwette, you have been charged with treason. You talked in the lectures and said things for them damn Chinese."

A chorus of yeas and snarls answered the leader. The leader quickly raised a hand for silence.

"You were known to have long meetings with the Chinese. Many of us were beaten for what we talked about when just us Americans were alone in the hut, and you squealed to them bastards. You are a snitch and sniveling coward. All these excuses about learning to read we know are a crock. If you couldn't read you wouldn't have passed the qualification test to enlist. You are guilty of treason."

A new chorus started but the leader raised his hand, again. He resumed. "It is the judgment of this court that you are not fit company for any of us. It has been decided that you will leave this ship."

Bert's eyes widened at the pronouncement. Off the ship? The meaning sank in. A gag in his mouth, his arms tied behind his back, pitch dark, and overboard. Then a weird calm came over Bert. No more shame about reading. No more Shirley Annes wanting to take his money. No worry about the army wanting him in a court martial. He was tired. His struggle ceased.

"All set?" was an angry question from the leader.

"No. Let me at the bastard." A hard blow hit Bert behind his ear. He saw shooting stars as a sharp pain like an electric shock exploded down his spine and into the top of his right leg.

"Hell, no. I want to mash his lying face in." A brief look at another snarling face then a fist hit Bert's mouth. He felt the blood as the fist drew back and hit again, this time on the nose. Bert's head snapped back. He snuffled involuntarily.

His wind was hammered from him as a fist hit his midsection. His knees buckled. Two strong arms held him up.

"Not yet, shithead. You don't go over till we've paid you back!" The blows came. Two sharp jabs to his ribs. Another hard fist to his head. It was black. The world was black, quiet, and he felt no more blows. He was being walked. To the rail? Was the cold water next? This must be the end.

A merciful quiet settled over Bert. Held up by two or three angry ex-POWs, his feet only touched the deck because of his long build. Both eyes swollen shut from fists of frustration, right leg almost as numb as his neck, Bert had left the angry mob.

His mind mercifully retreated from the troopship and the would be executioners. He was standing next to his Maw as his Paw's two millworker friends shoveled the rest of the dirt into his Paw's grave. He cried at the pathetic marker that was all to mark a life of hard struggle.

"Well, Bert," Maw said quietly, "he's gettin some rest and peace, now."

"Yes, Ma'm, I reckon so."

Maw put an arm around Bert's shoulder. "Don't want you a frettin' none 'bout Paw. I 'low's how he's at rest first time in his hard life."

She patted his shoulder as they walked from the little lonely group of headstones and turned up the road to their mill-house. He could still feel Maw's tender and loving embrace on his shoulders. Again came her words of encouragement that now sounded almost like an invitation.

"After all his struggle it's time fer him to rest. Worried 'bout a feedin' us all his life that I know. It's just rest now and wait fer Judgment Day."

A rude jolt as Bert felt his foot hit metal. The ships' rail. Well, he'd done the best he could with what life give him. Just a short time in the water then rest 'till Judgemednt Day. Rest in peace.

Loud noises. Other voices. Silence. He was still standing. Someone spoke harshly. New hands grabbed Bert around the chest. He couldn't open his eyes but could tell he was being walked a long way to the rail. His feet shuffled against metal, again. Was this the rail? Hot air. Stale air like a compartment. Inside? Bert tried to open his eyes. He could only see a glare of light. Then his hearing cleared.

"What's wrong, Padre?"

"This man's been beaten. A Kangaroo Kourt was going to throw him overboard. I want to leave him here while I get the medics."

"Let's take him back to one of the booths. One of the team is working and will keep an eye on him."

Bert was moving again or being moved. He could see from one eye. He was propelled down a short passage way to a small booth near the end of the passage. A GI in the cubicle stood from a folding desk.

"Sir?"

"Roy," the new officer spoke, "the Chaplain needs to let this man rest here while he gets the medics and a stretcher."

"Certainly, Sir." The other GI pulled a chair forward and Bert was eased into it. The Chaplain left and the other officer turned. "Bert, you're safe and can rest here. I'll man the entry." That officer left.

Bert looked at the other, a mere blur out of his worst eye now and tried to smile. The lip stung and he still snuffled through his nose.

The other guy smiled, "My name's Roy. Can I get you something while we wait? Coffee, maybe a beer?"

"No," Bert mumbled.

"I'd get you a wet cloth for that, ah, those places, but the medics will be here quickly."

The comment was answered only by silence.

"Would you like to talk, while we wait, I mean." Roy offered quietly.

"They..." Bert was silent for a minute, "they just started a whomping on me."

"I can see that," Roy responded easily.

"And," after a short silence, "they called me a traitor, they did."

"Called you what?" Roy asked.

"Them'sss tied me...them..."

The sentence was not finished. Roy waited.

"Bert?" Roy asked quietly. No response. "Bert?" a bit louder but still no response.

Bert did not hear Roy. So tired and hurt in so many places, worse than in the camp. It was cold there. Bert shivered. Shivered like in the hut when they took his blanket. Bert shivered now and began to slump when Roy caught him and lowered him to the floor of the cubicle. Bert continued to shake even more violently. Roy unbuttoned his fatigue jacket and covered Bert as much as he could.

Roy ran to the team office, "Mr. Burton," he called as he neared the office. "That guy passed out. Shock."

Chief Warrant Officer Burton picked up the hand set and cranked the phone. Just then three men in white coats pushed in from the outside. One wore captain's bars on his collar and a second carried a collapsible canvas stretcher.

"Down here, Sir." Roy led the way for the medics as he ran to the cubicle. The three medics squeezed in, placed the stretcher near Bert and began their work.

The captain knelt, quickly placed a hand alongside Bert's windpipe, and said to one of the medics with a pad and paper, "Got a pulse, breathing appears good." He looked up at Roy, "Any witness?"

"The officer who brought him in said he was beaten by fellow repatriates."

"Fists, clubs, what?"

"He didn't say, Sir," Roy answered.

117

"Was he alert when brought in? Could he speak?" The doctor looked at Roy.

"A few intelligible sentences, Sir, then began to shake and his speech slowed."

"Slowed or slurred?"

"Both, Sir, but the slur was not harsh, more like a soft lisp," Roy responded.

Careful not to move Bert's head, the Captain used tongue depressor and penlight to look in Bert's mouth, nose, and ears. He lifted the eyelids and flashed the penlight across the eyes a couple of times each.

"No evidence of bleeding here, possible contusion near the left eye." The doctor's practiced hands continued a careful examination of the neck, skull, and clavicle. The doctor looked over his shoulder at the note taker, "Go get x-ray set for a full spine series, stat. Oh, and set up an IV."

As the one corpsman left immediately, the doctor continued his examination with deft fingers. He moved probing digits along the shoulders, arms, along the rib cage, and down both legs.

"Possible fracture left rib cage." The doctor quickly removed Roy's fatigue blouse, rolled it tightly and placed it alongside Bert's neck. "Okay," he motioned to the other waiting corpsman, "Let's do a log roll."

The two rolled Bert onto his side with the rolled fatigue blouse now holding the head from any sag as the body lay on the side. The third corpsman returned in time to expand the stretcher and place it along side Bert's back and the three carefully rolled the stretcher and Bert back onto the deck.

The returned corpsman handed the doctor a tightly rolled towel which the doctor carefully placed on the side of Bert's neck opposite Roy's rolled fatigue blouse and stabilized the head.

"Cuff him for a B/P read while I check for pneumothorax," the captain directed as he placed his stethoscope at various places on Bert's lower chest. "Not too bad. Good pupil response, no obvious spinal injuries but x-ray will tell for sure. A lump behind his left ear will be checked for possible brain stem injury, lung sounds are good, bilateral."

With the completion of the examination, meaningless to Roy, the doctor motioned to the two corpsmen. "Up, up, and away. I'll monitor B/P and pulse as we go. Hi Ho, Silver."

The trio carefully threaded their way out of the Team Area.

෬ ෬ ෬

The next morning Roy entered the Team Office carrying his empty cup. "Good morning, Sir." Chief Burton nodded in response and raised his cup, "Coffee's good."

"Thank you," as he talked, Roy walked to the urn and drew a cup of coffee, "What's the word on our last night's guest, Sir?" he sipped gingerly from the hot coffee.

"Not sure, but I figured you'd want to visit him first thing this morning and report." Chief Burton continued at his desk work.

"Well, Sir," Roy blew again on his coffee. "Why, pray tell would I do that, or did I just receive a well disguised assignment?"

"We're beyond the twelve mile limit and therefore out of a war zone and I cannot have you shot for questioning an order," the Chief Warrant Officer paused to drink his now cool coffee. "Have a seat and I'll draw a picture."

Chief Burton was an experienced Counter Intelligence Corps Officer who had a proven knack of smelling investigative material. He worked well with the various agents with his off-hand manner. He was industrious, curious, and friendly. Roy had worked under his command previously in Japan.

Roy complied, "I hear and obey Great Chief, Sir."

"My you are a suspicious lout." Burton shook his head. "Visit the lad in the infirmary. Establish a good working relationship and solid rapport. I believe he'd have some good information in statements about his time with the Chinese. In particular I'd suggest some details of how the Chinese worked with him." Chief Burton paused for another mouthful of coffee. "In addition, for the record, is there any evidence to indicate the recipient of last night's surprise could be a plant as in planned for a long-term use?"

"How long was he north of the Yalu?" Roy was all business, now.

119

"Two and a half years."

"And last night's beating." Roy wanted background.

"Fellow repatriates who accuse him of collaboration."

"Sounds like statement territory to me, Sir."

ଔ   ଔ   ଔ

Bert returned to the world of the living slowly as if his body were awakening one part at a time. His eyes opened or at least one admitted light. With a tentative finger he explored the closed eye to find a bandage covered it.

"How are you feeling this morning, Corporal?"

Surprised at a female voice, Bert looked around the sides of his bed before noticing the starched khaki slacks at the head of his bed. "Ma'm?" He blinked the unbandaged eye.

"I want to take a look at your bandages, okay?" The nurse then stepped to the side of Bert's bed and began a careful analysis of the various bandages and ointments.

Bert touched the bandage on his eye. The nurse responded. "I want to let the doctor examine that one. There may only be swelling. He'll say what to do. He'll have reviewed the x-rays for tissue swelling and specific damage."

She continued the cursory examination as Bert lay in astonishment. A live round-eyed woman. He hadn't seen one for three years. He couldn't decide if she was really beautiful or he was overly impressed with the fact that she had round eyes and spoke clear English.

"Lip won't need stitches." She carefully examined both sides of Bert's head which remained stabilized with a block on each side. "Those bruises will go down. They'll look Technicolor by tomorrow but they'll start to heal." She looked at the chart on the headboard again then turned back to Bert.

"How do those ribs feel?"

"Oh, they's okay, I guess," was his slow response.

"Do something for me?" She smiled.

"Oh, yes, Ma'm." Whatever.

"Lie very still and take a deep breath." She watched his face as she laid a warm soft hand on his side and smiled. "Another deep breath."

This breath was accompanied by a sharp pain. Bert winced, and she frowned.

"We may have to take more x-rays but we'll let the doctor say. Need anything right now?"

"Oh, no Ma'm."

The nurse smiled and moved to another bed in the ward.

Left alone, Bert closed his one eye and sighed. He could almost feel the mess he was in slinking up on him even here. All the others really hated him. What had he done that they thought was so awful? How could he explain so they would understand? The lack of understanding was almost as troublesome as the pain from last night's beating.

He was lucky that officer came along to save him, wasn't he?

Bert thought of his paw. He remembered how his paw had struggled all his life to get a few dollars ahead for the family. Maw had said it was almost as hard on paw fretting about no money as the physical work at the mill was hard on him.

Was paw better off dead, now? Maw had said when they buried paw that at least his worries were over. If Bert had been thrown over the side last night would his worries be over?

"Hey, fellah, you awake?"

Bert was surprised out of his thoughts by the intrusion. He looked up to see a GI standing along side of his bed. "What?" was Bert's surprised answer.

"Just thought I'd stop by and see how you feel this morning."

"Well," Bert hesitated for a moment. "I guess I'm okay."

"I'm the guy you talked to. Last night the Chaplain brought you to my office to wait for the medics. You were pretty bumfuzzled, if you don't remember I can understand."

"Sorta remember, some."

"At least you're alert and talking this morning. I'll take that as good."

"I do feel some better, thanks."

"My name's Roy," he stuck out a hand to Bert. "Okay if I call you Bert?"

"Oh, sure," Bert took the offered hand and they shook.

"Do you know when you'll be up and about?"

"Doctor ain't come by yet. I don't rightly know." Bert answered.

"Well, when they let you up and you're feeling better, stop by and we can chat over some coffee. It gets tiresome while I'm on duty."

"Okay, Roy." Bert smiled.

Roy turned to leave then turned back, "Anything I can get you?"

"No, thanks."

"Don't forget, Bert," the departing Roy raised a hand. "Drop by for a chat."

Bert watched Roy leave and sighed, it was nice to talk to someone with no ax to grind and no beef to settle. Might be nice to sit and chat, friendly like.

Roy stopped at the desk near the exit from the ward and spoke to the nurse at the desk, "Excuse me, could you give me any information about Bert Cronwette, the guy they brought in last night?"

"Well, the x-rays indicated a severe bruise, left rib, no cardiac tamponade, and we have ruled out Beck's triad." Roy held up both hands defensively.

"Sorry, ma'm, I only wanted to know if he might be ambulatory in a day or so."

"Yes."

ભ   ભ   ભ

A few days later, Bert tapped at the open end of the cubicle.

"Hey," Roy greeted him.

Bert responded in kind.

"Come in the house."

"You busy?" Bert smiled.

"Naw, just collecting bellybutton fuzz. Come on in."

Bert slowly bent into the only other chair in the cubicle, "Thanks. I's a bit peaked and puny feeling."

"Well, you must be feeling better, the medics have you ambulatory, I see." Roy pointed to Bert's right foot. "That slight limp from the camp or the other night?"

"Doctor says it may be from the visit from my friends. He can't say yet if it'll go way or not. All in all, I's a bit stiff and sore, but able to sit up and take medicine."

"Hey, can I get you anything? Coffee? Soda?"

"I'd be obliged for coffee...if...we don't hafta go in the big mess hall."

"I was thinking of having a cup on the Team's separate mess deck. Okay?"

"I guess."

Over coffee the two chatted like old friends checking up on each other's life. Some questions clearly indicated Bert's almost three years in the camps kept him totally away from the events that had passed in the world.

"What's television?"

"What's a bikini?"

"The POW Olympics didn't make the papers?"

"General MacArthur was replaced?"

Roy answered those he could which usually led to more questions.

"The Chinese POWs rioted in Cheju Do?"

"Was the Chinese POWs being treated badly?"

"I don't think so. It seems the Chinese got a couple of their political leaders captured, on purpose. The leaders organized the POWs and rioted. Killed some of their fellow POWs who wouldn't cooperate. Snatched an American General who tried to talk to them and held him for ransom," Roy explained.

"He get away?"

"The 187th Air-Borne went in and broke it up."

"The Chinese didn't say nothing about that. They sure don't like to...ah...lose face, that's it. Don't lose face."

"I reckon they don't."

"But we thought the Olympics would be in the headlines. They was a lot of reporters there and them picture guys."

"They were probably Third World news media."

"Where's that Third World?" Bert puzzled.

"The newspapers always say there's the democratic world, you know, America and England. They say there's the Communist World, and the Third World. The smaller countries that are not always on America's and England's side are supposed to be a Third World," Roy explained.

"Little guy's always in the middle, like?" Bert queried.

"That's about right."

Bert sat still for a few minutes, drained his coffee, shrugged, and issued some home-grown but accurate philosophy. "Little guys always get squeezed in the middle, like between two bullies, don't they?"

Chapter 9

Statements

The next day, over coffee in the Team's small mess deck, Roy and Bert worked over specific questions about the camp. Roy kept his questions to the activities in the camp except when Bert mentioned Todd.

"This Todd, you say he was on the troop ship with you and also in the 24th Division?"

"Yes, we even did six days of KP together on that ship." Bert offered.

"Did you know his name, his last name?"

"Well, I's not too sure but I think it was McCoy or something like that." Bert decided.

"McCoy? You mean like Hatfield and McCoy?" Roy suppressed a smile, but got no response from Bert. "Any idea where he came from in the States?"

"Think he talked 'bout Tennessee, in the hills there. I don't remember him a saying nothing 'bout any hats in the field." Bert shook his head slightly.

"Did any of the other POWs say anything about him possibly being a snitch?"

"No," Bert perked up a bit at the question. "And I 'member askin' him one time why they was all so sure I was tatlin' to the Chinks and no one ever suspected him?"

"What was his answer?"

"Well, first off, he didn't answer straight away. You see he's always lettin' his hair hang down over his face 'n never shaved. When I asked 'bout him getting extra food regular and no other POW worrin' that, he smiled and said it's 'cause he didn't talk out and let all them other poor bastards hear him to know that he's talkin'." Bert shrugged.

"He was sneaky?"

"Yea, that's it." Bert sat up straighter in his chair, "I 'member now. He said that he helped them Chineemen by listening and telling the Chinks things they wanted to know but that he stayed in the back of things and nobody noticed him. Me, he said I talked in class and everybody heard me." Bert almost smiled, "Yea, that's the difference he said. Nobody thought of him cause they didn't see him or hear him."

"And he went to China?" Roy checked.

"Sure did, and wanted me to go with 'em." Bert added along with a nod of his head."

"Why didn't you?" Roy asked. "Surely you knew the army would court martial you? And some told you they would see that you got yours."

"I didn't think learning to read was bad." Bert toyed with his coffee cup for a minute and added. "I still don't see why."

"Did you ever talk with Todd about Communism?" Roy asked.

"He only talked about them Chineemen and not any o' their ideas."

"I see." Roy sat a minute before he probed further. "Can you give me an example of how he talked about the Chinese?"

"Sure," Bert shrugged a slim shoulder. "He's sayin' he started being nice and telling them Chineemen things they wanted to hear as soon as he got there."

"He never said anything about the Chinese way of life or why he started helping them?" Roy pursued the ideological possibilities.

"No. All he ever said was him tellin' them about what the POWs were sayin' and plannin' so's the Chineemen would give him more food and them long-johns."

"Long-johns?" Roy was puzzled.

"Yea. He showed me his brand new woolen long-johns. That's just this last winter," Bert explained.

"US Army or quilted Chinese?" Roy double-checked.

126

"Oh, I touched them. They's good American all right."

"And he wanted you to go to China with him?" Roy checked again.

"I said no, but all he talked about was how he hated the US Army and that the Chineemen told him he'd live free and have women in China." Bert shook his head.

❧ ❧ ❧

Late afternoon sun glinted through a porthole into the Team Office. A small bit of that sun glinted down the passage where Bert sought Roy.

At the cubicle, he greeted Roy, "Hey, Roy. I ain't bothering anything?" Bert checked.

"No, all statements are taken, all materials packed and stowed in preparation for docking tomorrow. Just came by to collect a few personal things, come on in the house." Roy waved a hand at a chair.

"What you gonna do after you get home, Roy?"

"I guess once the army is through with me I'll teach."

Bert was surprised. "Teach, like in a school?"

"Sure. I taught part of a semester the year before I was drafted. I think I'll like working with high school-age students."

"It don't seem like you'd be a teacher." Bert puzzled.

"Why not?"

"Well, for one thing you don't always go 'round correctin' people when they make mistakes like me. That's what teachers do."

"I don't think always correcting people is the best way to help them. I noticed you said that Sergeant England was working with you on your use of words. Have you forgotten his effort?" Roy smiled.

"I guess I have. In the camps nobody gave a hoot how you talked." A bitter laugh. "They sure did get out 'a joint 'bout what you said, though. Then, when I got to Freedom Gate they said they ain't had any information from 24th Division about me a makin' sergeant. I guess all that was just some shit they's throwin'. I don't

127

reckon it was England's fault." Another shrug of the thin shoulders. "Where it looks like they's gonna send me, a stripe ain't gonna make no never mind. They may be waiting for me at the dock."

"I wish I could say, Bert. I know that waiting for a bad thing to happen and not knowing when can be worst of all."

"Sure 'nuff." Bert's reply was a bit laconic.

"Your wait may be a long one. They'll probably extend your enlistment 'till they make a decision. All the statements have to be reviewed, investigations conducted as warranted, and a decision by the area commander about a trial," Roy explained.

"That could be a long time, huh?" Bert queried.

"Up to a year of waiting, I'm afraid, Bert."

"I'll just do what I can," Bert drawled.

"Be on your toes. The same guys who wanted to throw you overboard that first night are not the only ones who think they have a right to tear into you, some way. Many have already decided you're guilty." Roy warned.

After a minute of silence, Bert stood, smiled a wan smile, and put out his hand. "Thank you, Roy. Good luck with your teachin'."

"No problem, Bert, and good luck to you in all things." They shook hands.

ෆ ෆ ෆ

For Bert the long bus ride across the United States from San Francisco was a rehearsal time for a homecoming meeting with maw. It was about as Bert thought it would be when he sat with maw the first night at home.

"Bert." Maw's face was solemn and the wrinkles showed from a life of drudgery and almost three years of worry. "I gonna ask, all those things in the newspapers and all. Did you do what it says in them papers?"

"No, Maw."

She looked relieved for a second then the frown returned. "How come it is they say you did?"

He looked at his half-finished glass of milk for a long minute then faced his truth. "I always felt bad that I can't read. In school I's always called dumb. But not learnin' and readin' wasn't that I didn't try. I kept tryin' but nothin' happened."

A silence on his part was interrupted only by his mother's tender smile and nod.

"It always hurt that I couldn't answer them questions in class. Then I did good in the army. I was good in training and while I's on the line. Then in that camp them Chinese found I could read some words. They gave me things that I could read. I could answer them questions the officer asked me. I could read. I knew them answers, good." He paused and looked at Maw.

"I was so happy and I wanted them others to know I could read. The officer he let me read these things and when he asked questions in class. I could answer. I could prove that I could read."

Maw smiled in spite of the tears in her eyes.

"Maw, I just ain't got the words to tell how good it felt for the first time in my life to answer them questions. When I stood up that first time it was like, well even though Jock and them others wasn't there, it's like telling them I could read. And tellin' them I's no dummy."

There was a moment of silence then Maw squeezed Bert's hand. "I love you son. I never put no stock in them stories in the papers. You done the best. When you go back to soldiering you keep doing the best you can."

"Yes, Ma'm."

Chapter 10

Pre-Trial

Bert reported to Headquarters Command, Fort Sam Houston, Texas. Master Sergeant William Brinkley, Company First Sergeant, Headquarters Company, told Orderly Room Clerk Private First Class James Q. Randall, to show Bert to his assigned quarters.

Once Randall had departed with Bert, Sergeant Brinkley made two phone calls. First, per his instructions, he called the Provost Marshall's Office (PMO). He reported to the PMO that Corporal Cronwette had just signed in. The second call relayed the same information to Headquarters Commandant, base facility's commanding officer.

Bert set his duffel bag in a corner of the small assigned cadre room. He opened the window and lay back on his cot. He loosened his tie and tried to relax. He was prepared for a wait. He was surprised when the clerk appeared at the door and told him to report to the orderly room.

Sergeant Brinkley was waiting in the outer office.

"Corporal Cronwette, you are to report to the PMO representative in my office."

Bert's heart sank as he walked into the office, saluted, and reported. "Corporal Cronwette reporting as directed, Sir."

Two officers were at the First Sergeant's desk, one a captain, and the other, a second lieutenant, stood nearby. Both wore side-arms.

"Corporal, it is my duty to inform you that you are charged with violation of Articles 104 and 105 of the Uniform Code of Military Justice. These two violations did occur while you were a

130

Prisoner of War and held in Camp 5, Yalu, Manchuria."

Bert was in a daze of resignation and confusion as the captain read Bert's rights as indicated in Article 31 of the UCMJ. When he had finished with the military equivalent of the rights guaranteed under the 5th Amendment to the Constitution, the captain paused and looked up.

"Do you have any questions or wish to make a statement at this time?"

"When will this trial be, Sir?"

"A trial date has not yet been set. You are to understand that although you are charged but not officially considered guilty pending the decision of the General Court, you will be confined to your quarters. An officer will be appointed as your defense. Should you wish, you may hire a private attorney, however the cost of such attorney will not be paid by the government. Any other questions?"

"No, Sir."

"Please report to the first sergeant for any further instructions regarding your conditions here."

Bert saluted, about faced, and marched to the outer office.

"Confinement to quarters will continue until after trial and judgement by the appointed Board of Officers," Sergeant Brinkley explained. "Mail is regular. Within this building are the day room, this orderly room, mess hall, and company billets. You may not leave the building without permission of the duty officer. Even then you must be accompanied by the duty officer, or an authorized representative identified by the duty officer. Any request to leave the quarters must be made in advance. You will inform either the duty officer or designee of your location any time you leave your room other than to go to the latrine. You will not be entered on the duty roster. You will stand all inspections in quarters." The sergeant paused and looked at Bert. "Questions?"

The response was flat. "No."

Back in his small room Bert loosened his tie again and sat back on his bunk. Bert Cronwette's long wait began.

ognition ognition ognition

The tall Women Army Corps (WAC) pushed open the door in response to Colonel Rudyard Kipling Simpson's terse, "Come."

"Colonel, Sir, a..." The major general she was trying to announce pushed past her into the office.

"C'mon, Rudy. Get out from behind that damn desk."

Colonel Simpson stood surprised for a second, saluted, and stepped from behind his desk. "General Staunton, Sir. Glad to see you."

Simpson nodded past the general and the WAC left, quietly closing the door.

"Gawdamit, always at your desk. No wonder Patton didn't think you worth a shit."

A broad grin spread across Simpson's face and the two shook hands warmly. Simpson and Staunton had roomed together at West Point and graduated numbers six and seven in the Class of '36. Both arrived in North Africa in Operation Husky, 1942. Their careers followed each other, keeping apace till near the end of the war. Staunton got two promotions and his BG above Simpson at the Battle of the Bulge. Staunton was in the right place at the right time. He had been Division G-3, Training and Plans, when the Division Command Post took direct hits from German artillery. Both the CG and ADC were KIA. Subsequent to Patton moving Staunton to Division ADC, he earned his second star just before V-E Day.

"What brings a war horse like you out of hiding, Chauncy?"

"Quick business then back to Washington for an 0730 hours meeting with the Marine Corps Commandant."

"Sounds like serious business."

"It is." The General looked around, "Say, how about a cool one? Your quarters, maybe?"

Colonel Simpson buzzed to call his car around. At Colonel Simpson's quarters, General Staunton performed the social amenities with Mrs. Simpson, and at General Staunton's hint, the two officers retreated to the Colonel's small study with drinks in hand.

"This all seems a bit cloak-and-daggerish, Chauncy?"

"We need to be most discreet, Rudy. It's been decided that POW Cronwette will be charged under Articles 104 and 105. You'll preside."

"Well," Simpson hesitated a minute possibly considering the previous information that the Army Area Commander was to make that decision. "I didn't know."

"You were told that your Fourth Army CG would make the decision. The problem isn't that simple. In order to bring pressure to bear on the Marines to get after their fly-boy who shot off his face about germ warfare, the Pentagon decided to get after Cronwette in a big way."

"Oh." Silence as they each sipped their drinks.

"The personal trip is to get a drink out of you, and to make sure you as presiding officer of the board know the gravity of the situation."

"I see."

"We have one senator in DC finding commies under every desk in the Pentagon. Another senator has his teeth into that idiot general taking a private with connections for joy rides in the idiot's staff plane."

"I heard about that. Two classes ahead of us, wasn't he?"

"Should have been found and booted before his first full year. The point is," General Staunton continued, "we have to prove to the media and the senate that the army is no Mama's House. Those who violate the UCMJ will be punished. No coddling of any dumb-ass whether he can read or not."

"I understand."

"You'll have some help at least with the media coverage. A special effort was made to appoint Lieutenant Bartles to the court."

"Oh, yes. The hold-out POW."

General Staunton nodded and stood, "I need a ride to Randolph Field. Busy hands, you know."

"My car waited." Colonel Simpson offered.

"Good, Oh, I almost forgot, about your star." General Staunton remembered.

"Yes?"

"You're on the current list. Don't want it to look like a set-up,

133

and we tried to push it through on the last list but didn't catch it before it got to the Congressional Affairs Office. This list is not expected to hit any bumps."

ଓ ଓ ଓ

Colonel Simpson, G-1, Personnel, Fourth Army, received his orders naming him Presiding Officer and the list of Officers and the one enlisted man to serve on the Board. Colonel Simpson immediately set the wheels of military justice in motion. He scheduled an informal meeting with the two named Officers, Captain Fred I. Goines, Defense, and Second Lieutenant Wendell H. Lawson, Judge Advocate General's Office, to prosecute. Prior to scheduling a pre-trial conference with the two, Colonel Simpson carefully reviewed the requests and particularly the defense requests.

ଓ ଓ ଓ

A 1941 Ford eased to the end of the Fourth Army Headquarters' Visitor parking space. The driver gathered his hat and papers as he slid from the car. He donned his hat and walked up the sidewalk. He returned the salute from the MP at the gate to the Old Quadrangle. The captain wondered as he entered the old structure if the Fourth Army continued to use the old original fort for public relations or was the CG a history buff?

Sure as he had been told, a right turn placed him under the sign, "Chief of Personnel, Fourth Army." Captain Goines opened the door, doffed his hat, and strode to the desk behind which sat a scowling buck sergeant vision fixed on a paper in front of him. When the Captain was about to clear his throat, the sergeant looked up.

"Sir?"

"Good morning, Sergeant. I have a ten hundred hours appointment with Colonel Simpson. I'm Captain Goines."

"Yes, Sir. If you'll have a seat, please. The Colonel will see you and Lieutenant Lawson shortly."

Goines turned in the direction indicated, saw an effete and ramrod second lieutenant, and extended a hand as he approached.

"Hello, I'm Fred Goines, appointed defense for Corporal Cronwette."

The young Lieutenant quickly extended a limp and moist hand. "Yes, Sir. Wendell Lawson, JAG."

Goines was wary. "Then you're a real lawyer?"

"Yes, Sir. Baylor, class of '51." The young lieutenant smiled eagerly.

"Baylor?" Goines reflected thoughtfully a moment then his face brightened. "Waco. Yes, Baylor University."

"Yes, Sir. I..."

"Gentlemen," interrupted the sergeant, "Colonel Simpson is waiting."

Without further words the two marched in and saluted. Simpson returned the salutes and waved them to two chairs in the small, cramped office. One penalty the Fourth Army staff paid for the commanding general's insistence on use of the old nineteenth century fort as Fourth Army Headquarters was their existence in small uncomfortable office space.

Simpson had remained seated and looked first at the Captain. "I believe you are Captain Goines?"

"Yes, Sir."

"And Lieutenant Lawson." The Colonel finished the recognitions as he referred to a printed sheet on his desk.

"Sir."

"Gentlemen, the trial date is 30 April. Any problems?"

"Sir, may the defense request a later date?"

"Certainly, provided justification is shown, Captain."

"The defense wishes to call two witnesses, both from out of state."

"Travel-time a problem?"

"Yes, Sir."

"The nature of their testimony?"

"One is the accused's platoon leader from Korea, and the..."

"Excuse me, Captain, was this platoon leader in the POW Camp when the alleged violations occurred?"

"No, Sir, but..."

"Regrettably, Captain, the only certifiable witness would have to have been present in the camp and prepared to testify as a witness to the act or acts specified to have taken place. If those circumstances do not pertain, the motion is denied."

"I understand, Sir, but the implication of cowardice by aiding and abetting can be refuted by the witness to combat behavior and leadership actions."

"There is no charge of cowardice." Colonel Simpson raised a shoulder to emphasize his reason for denial.

"Yes, the Colonel is correct." The lieutenant smiled coyly as he curried strokes. "Cowardice is part of an article not included in these charges."

Goines couldn't help a side glance at Lawson whom he may have recognized as a twit.

"Let me explain, Captain," began Col. Simpson. "The specific charge has to do only with the behavior while held captive by the enemy. Any behavior before or since his captivity is not material to the specification or charge. It cannot be allowed into evidence." The colonel waited.

Captain Goines sat in temporary befuddlement. What now? None of the other POWs' statements were favorable or in any way supportive of Cronwette. The teacher.

"Sir, the statements by Cronwette clearly indicate his reading problem. That was, of course, true while he was in the enemy camp. The trickery of the Chinese using that fact is one area to which testimony is available from Cronwette's school teacher. She is the other witness I request." Goines smiled confidently.

"Was she in the camps?" inquired the younger officer.

Goines looked again at the JAG Lieutenant. What a little twit, a porch-climbing twit to boot. He ignored Lieutenant Twit and pressed his request.

"The point of her testimony, Colonel, is the reading problem that existed before, during, and today. It was the compelling reason that made Cronwette susceptible to the captor's blandishments about solving the reading problem."

"I see, Captain. And what are the teacher's expertise and

credentials?" asked Colonel Simpson.

"She is licensed and state certified, Sir."

"She must have one of two qualifications to meet the requirements of the UCMJ." The Colonel enumerated. "Be certified as a reading specialist who administered an appropriate instrument that identified his reading problem, or, of course, been present in the camp."

Goins sat in utter defeat. Then a sudden flash of insight must have registered with the captain because he raised a questioning hand.

"Captain?" Colonel Simpson nodded.

"Is it my correct understanding that an investigation has been ongoing to include written statements taken from the witnesses in the camps?"

"You are correct." The colonel nodded.

"I request access to those statements and the investigative reports, Sir."

"Oh, the reports would be classified," interrupted the JAG's resident twit.

Goines glanced at the beaming face and was probably rewarded with the flash impression of a canine retriever who had just dropped a bird at his master's feet.

"What the lieutenant suggests may be true. Be that as it may, such would be out of my authority to request, Captain. You may, however wish to contact the Operations Office of the 112th CIC Detachment for an answer."

"I see." Goines was completely shaken at the roadblock.

"Does the JAG have any questions or motions?" Simpson looked at the lieutenant.

"None, Sir."

"Thank you for your time, Lieutenant." The colonel smiled.

A bit surprised when he finally recognized his dismissal, the young JAG quickly stood, saluted, and left the office.

"Captain Goines, I'm going to have a cup of coffee. Will you please join me?"

"Oh, yes, Sir. Thank you, Sir." Goines, crestfallen at the defeat of his hopes, smiled nevertheless.

The colonel reached for the intercom on his desk, toggled the switch, and asked for coffee. The sergeant from the desk in the outer office entered almost instantly with a tray, two cups, and an insulated server. He sat the tray on the desk and stood to attention.

"Thank you, Sergeant." The colonel smiled as he added, "Hold my calls."

The sergeant left as Simpson poured coffee for himself and motioned at Goines. "Please help yourself."

While Goines poured coffee in the second cup, Colonel Simpson carried his cup to the chair vacated by Lawson, and sat.

"Captain, I'll be frank. You're in a most thankless situation. It's standard procedure for non-legally trained officers to be detailed the defense of enlisted personnel charged under the UCMJ. I fully appreciate, from experience, how it feels to defend a man with seemingly no weapons. I empathize that both the platoon leader in Korea and almost any good teacher would provide excellent testimony as to his bravery and the reading problem, if allowed under the UCMJ."

Colonel Simpson paused and sipped from his cup then continued.

"There are many good points that either, as a witness, could make in defense of the accused's character and problems. We are, however, bound to the rules as set forth by the UCMJ. It is specific on the qualifications of a witness."

Again the colonel paused to sip his coffee. "I know your frustration at not being able to provide what to you is a logical defense. By reading each article carefully and combing through, point-by-point each specification, you'll be doing your best."

"I'm sorry, Sir. I'm not sure I see that as any help." The frown on Goines' face punctuated his quandary.

"Captain," Simpson pointed to the left breast pocket of Goins' uniform. "I see you wear the CIB, the Combat Infantry Badge. European Theatre?"

"Yes, Sir. Ninth Division, Sir." Goins responded a bit dismayed by the apparent change of subject.

"For purposes of making my point let me pose a hypothetical situation. Given a mission to neutralize an enemy position, what would be your first activities?" The colonel waited.

"Well," Goines began slowly, thinking. "I'd collect all the dope G-2 and G-3 had available particularly as to any special features of the position, its strong points, and hopefully, its weak points, Sir."

"Exactly, Captain."

"But, Sir..." Goines ended his protest when the Colonel raised a hand.

"Do the same, now. Use that careful analysis of each article's strong points, weak points, and possible approaches to defend against it. Plan to concentrate your defense on those areas of the articles that seem most promising to your success." Colonel Simpson waited.

"Carefully analyze each point of each article, each charge, and each specification?" Goines asked.

"Specifically your task is to root out any and all discrepancies and use them to defend this soldier. That's the challenge."

"And, aside from that I'm pretty well hamstrung." Goines sighed.

"In a nutshell, Captain." Simpson offered a smile.

"But, Sir, what good is an appointed defense if there is no defense?" Goines pointed out.

"The search for errors in the article, in the specifications, and statements as they relate to the accused's activities is the defense." The colonel raised a finger for emphasis. "Remember, the statements taken on the ship from Inchon have been carefully reviewed and analyzed by both intelligence and JAG representatives. Inappropriate or incomplete statements were eliminated. A separate agency conducted a thorough investigation including additional interviews as appropriate. Only after all data was compiled were the decisions made." Colonel Simpson paused for a drink from his cup.

"Certainly sounds cautious and thorough," mused Captain Goines.

"Yes, Captain. A court martial is only scheduled and the charges presented to the accused after clear evidence is present that the UCMJ has been violated. The task of the defense is a last step in the constant chain of reviews to assure that justice is done." Simpson drained his cup of coffee and smiled.

ଔ ଔ ଔ

First Lieutenant Ramon L. Patencio pushed through the door to the BOQ unit he shared with Captain Goines. It was 1800 hours. Goines hunched over a desk covered with books, scribbled notes, and wads of paper, groused to himself.

"Take ten." Patencio announced.

The grumble became audible. "I wish."

"Boy, you are a mess. Nose to the grindstone. Just won't do, Captain," Patencio chided.

"Hell," Goines finally looked up. "I see no choice."

"Now which is it. Hots for the Flower of Baylor Law School or you just given up on cowgirl loving?"

"I have a fullbird on my ass. Colonels have a striving to become generals. Captains don't make major by pissing off future generals." Goines glared at his roommate.

"Oh, going regular army or just candyass, El Capitan?"

Patencio began a dance around the small room to his own nasal twang imitation of any local San Antonio or Central Texas honky tonk singer of the '50s doing some tear-jerking guitar ballad.

> Oh yes, out on Old Route 90 East,
> The Barn is swinging without rest,
> All them hungry farmers' daughters,
> Wanting to get their oughters.

As the parody continued, Goines only shook his head, "No chance tonight, Buddy."

"Oh, shit. Wake up." The dance pantomime ended. "Look, they don't even convene a court martial unless they got the cabrone cold seven ways from Sunday."

Patencio stood, hands on hips to continue. "All that poor bastard can do is get ready to see the priest 'cause his ass belongs to the Army's executioner."

Silence reigned for a minute before Goines turned back to his

140

desk with a shoulder shrug. "I know but I gotta try."

It was just after 23:30 hours when the conversation resumed as Patencio literally fell into the BOQ. A tired Goines helped the muttering drunk into bed and sat back at the desk. Goines rubbed his eyes and face and then looked at the desk. Resigned, he turned out the desk lamp and flopped into his own bed.

Into the collecting silence, Patencio muttered a few enduring phrases, probably from his strike-out at the Barn, and began to snore. Goines turned over and fell into his own needed sleep.

It was late the next morning when Goines finally got his badly hung-over roommate to the Fort Sam Officer's Club for breakfast. Goines asked for a couple of eggs, over-easy, toast, and coffee.

"Please, my love," Patencio smiled at the plump middle aged waitress. "Two soft-scrambled, dry toast, tomato juice, two aspirin, black coffee, some grits, and at least one cluck of your tongue and an effort at sincere sympathy." He tried to smile as he finished.

"Get ya the eggs, toast, juice, coffee, and grits. For the rest, you're on your own, Buster." With that the waitress was gone.

"Boy," Patencio grumped. "What is the world coming to when a good honest Don Juan can't even get a kind word?"

"You get no kind words from me just because you struck-out." Goines smiled.

"Hey. What do you mean, struck out?" Patencio pained.

The coffee was delivered quietly and the two began the stirring ritual, Patencio picked up the sugar first. Befuddled with his hang-over, Patencio found it difficult to execute any effective eye-hand-spoon-coffee coordination. Goines watched, trying to be patient. When the second spoon of sugar went mostly on the table, Goines snorted.

"Okay. Don't hold it all day."

"Not holding long," grumped Patencio.

"How long is hold, you sot?" Goines would have continued his complaint except that a thought was forming. "Hold? How long is hold?"

"Okay. Don't go into some weird tango, Compadre." Patencio pushed the sugar bowl across the table.

Goines stood. He looked unseeingly into the distance, then grabbed his hat and turned to leave.

"Hey. Where you going? Here's the damn sugar." Patencio called.

All he got from a fast departing roommate was a wave of the Captain's hand as he pushed rapidly toward the O Club exit.

CB CB CB

Colonel Simpson had made preparations for his part in the trial of Corporal Cronwette. He had toured almost all of the unused and out-of-the-way spots on the Fort Sam Houston Reservation that had facilities possibly suited to house the trial that also met his own particular specifications.

Lieutenant Colonel Battencourt, Assistant Quartermaster, Fourth Army, had identified all the possible locations based on Colonel Simpson's' previously outlined needs. Now the two were at the unused classrooms that had previously housed the expanded teaching facilities for Brooke Army Medical School. The temporary buildings were all one story, wooden structures. With the Korean War over and the expansion of the military temporarily halted, the teaching activities at Brookes had been drastically reduced. These small classroom buildings were available.

"This is it, Colonel," a reflected pause, "with some special preparation," Simpson added.

Battencourt pulled a small pad and pencil from his tunic pocket. "Yes, Sir?"

Colonel Simpson stood in the middle of the hot stuffy room and surveyed it critically. His eye carefully covered the details.

"Table for the Board, here." Simpson pointed to the end of the room nearest the small office and teaching-aid preparation room door. "Defense table here, AG here, and Law Officer and recorder tables to this side." He again looked at the floor plan he envisioned.

"The rest folding chairs, Sir?" Battencourt paused to make

more notes as directed.

"Only need about a dozen extra chairs. Only five media representatives will be authorized," Simpson mused aloud.

"Fans, Sir?"

"Oh, one at the back wall near the last window."

"The air is still and hot, I can provide more fans and have the room aired out a day or two in advance, Sir." Battencourt offered.

"Negative, Colonel. Have it cleaned up, chairs and tables in place, then locked up. Not to be opened till 0730 hours the morning of the trial," Simpson directed.

"It will be very hot and stuffy, Sir," the Quartermaster Officer offered in some disbelief.

"The last week in April? I'm counting on it being uncomfortable."

As Simpson finished his response he walked into the small adjoining room. A confused and uncertain Battencourt followed.

"One small table here," he pointed. "Coffee and rolls. No chairs. No fan." He smiled at Battencourt.

"I can do that, Sir." Battencourt had to add, again, "It will be very uncomfortable, Sir."

"Comfortable boards tend to languish over decisions, Colonel. I want us to convene, listen to arguments, decide, and get on with the day's work." Colonel Simpson strode from the room seeking his own fresh air and comfort.

Chapter 11

And Justice for All

At precisely 0800 hours, Colonel Rudyard K. Simpson, President of the General Court, Headquarters Fourth Army, Fort Sam Houston, Texas, led the other members of the appointed court into the hot, stuffy courtroom. From Colonel Simpson's previous instructions, the law officer was ready to move the proceedings sharply to conclusion.

Colonel Simpson noted with satisfaction as he took his chair at the middle of the assembling Board that the laboring floor fan had little or no impact on the stuffy room. He made a mental note to express his appreciation to Battencourt for his efficiency.

Major Tidwell F. Smathers, Law Officer, stood, straightened his tunic, picked up a sheaf of papers, and watched to see when the members of the court were in place. He cleared his throat and thus stilled the slight murmur of the few spectators. Second Lieutenant Wendell H. Lawson, representing the Judge Advocate General (JAG), along with Captain Goines, appointed defense, and Corporal Cronwette all rose.

Cronwette had been prepared by Capt. Goines for a long and boring time. Just before the Court had entered, Goines had reminded him. "The military court is a tedious thing, Bert. They're slow and will put you in mind of a snail's race. Every item must be covered in the prescribed way, sometimes twice. Some things will be read over and over. Just sit quietly. I'll tell you when to stand or speak."

Bert stood now and looked straight ahead.

"Attention to orders." The Law Officer opened the Court Martial.

The required reading of the General Order naming the members of the court followed. The charges and the specifications associated with those charges were read as well as the two Articles of the Uniform Code of Military Justice (UCMJ) with which Cronwette was charged of having violated while a Prisoner of War in the years 1951, 1952, and 1953, in the Chinese POW Camp, Manchuria.

The penalties available to the court to assess should they find the defendant guilty of the charges were read. Next the official Summary of Information concerning the statements and the resulting investigation was read. With the preambles completed the packet of materials was delivered to the President of the Court. The Law Officer then returned to his seat.

Colonel Simpson officially charged the members of the court. He next presented the pro forma challenge of pre-judgement to the members. "If any member of this court knows of any reason or circumstance to prevent him from rendering a clear and unbiased verdict, please make such information known to the court at this time."

"Sir." First Lieutenant Bartles, stood at his chair at the end of the Board table.

"Lieutenant Bartles, do you wish to address the court?" Colonel Simpson did not look to see who spoke. The procedure had been discussed with the young hero of the Korean War previously.

The young officer marched front and center to face the Presiding Officer. His ribbons and military decorations included the Bronze Star, with "V" clasp for valor, Distinguished Service Ribbon, Purple Heart, United Nations Service Ribbon, Korean Service Ribbon, and at the top of this display, the Combat Infantry Badge. Around his neck a red, white, and blue ribbon suspended the Congressional Medal of Honor just on top of the third button on his tunic.

"The lieutenant respectfully wishes to be excused from this court, Sir." The young officer stood ram-rod straight as he delivered his statement.

"Your reason?" intoned Simpson.

"The lieutenant respectfully informs the court that in the opinion of the lieutenant, the cowardly little son of a bitch should be summarily hung, Sir."

"The member is excused with the best wishes of the Court." Colonel Simpson's response was clearly heard even over the furious scribbling of notes by the media representatives. To the press this was headline stuff. Bartles, national hero, wounded, captured, imprisoned in a POW camp, had led a continuing campaign to thwart efforts by his captors at interrogation, and the resulting foul and inhumane treatment. Bartles saluted, executed a smart about face, and marched from the room. Behind him scuttled the Associated Press representative with notepad in hand. At his departure, quiet returned to the room.

One of the members of the Court, Lieutenant Colonel Battencourt, had looked curiously at Cronwette. A frown sat uneasily on Battencourt's brow. He looked at Cronwette as if trying to place an oddly familiar face. Battencourt's hand reached toward his tie, not a conscious need but an ingrained habit when under stress.

Cronwette looked up at the Court. His eyes swept to Battencourt. A telling moment of eye-contact. The accused let his gaze drop away from the coward he recognized.

Battencourt's lips parted slightly in shock. The frown was replaced by a look of stunned recognition. Battencourt looked suddenly ill. His face drained of color. One hand struggled momentarily with his tie. The lieutenant colonel looked intently at the papers in front of him on the table. A hand, again acting in ingrained habit of nervousness, reached toward his tie. Eyes forward but not focused on the papers on the table, he tried to shuffle idly with the papers which suddenly ended in his lap. Battencourt ignored the dropped papers. His hands lay limply in his lap.

Sweat formed on the officer's face. He pulled a handkerchief from a tunic pocket and blotted his face and neck. Unaware of Lieutenant Colonel Battencourt's apparent struggle and discomfort, the military proceedings moved forward.

Each of the Articles of which Cronwette was charged with

having violated was read and Cronwette responded not guilty to each. The JAG Officer entered into evidence various statements taken from returned POWs. He presented the Summary of Information of the resulting investigation. The JAG Officer stated the visits by Cronwette to the interrogation hut just prior to the indoctrination sessions in which Cronwette answered questions by making statements detrimental to the United States and its way of life was evidence of "holding intercourse with the enemy."

"These acts so described do violate Article 104, in that Corporal Cronwette did hold intercourse with the enemy and is therefore guilty as charged and therefore subject to the penalty of death."

"The defense may respond to the stated charge relative to Article 104." The law officer sat back down.

Captain Goines stood, almost smiled at Colonel Simpson, turned to the law officer and quietly dropped a bombshell. "The defense moves for dismissal of all charges and specifications under Article 104." The Captain's effort and late hours paid dividends.

"Grounds?" The Young JAG's voice almost cracked in surprise. "What grounds?"

"Hold, Sir," Goines responded calmly. "The wording of Article 104 is to hold intercourse with the enemy."

"And?" The young JAG demanded.

"Article 104, specifically sub-paragraph 2, deals with holding intercourse with the enemy. The word hold refers to an extended period of time. To continue intercourse over an extended period of time is not substantiated by any statements of evidence as presented," Goines summarized.

Goines continued despite a buzz from among the few press representatives. "The accused, in his sworn statement agrees that he did orally answer questions on two different occasions. Defense does stipulate that those two instances did take place. One after each of two separate visits to the Chinese officer. However, his sworn statement corroborated by the statements of others, is that after the second instance he was forcibly made aware that he should not participate in activity with the Chinese Officer. In following indoctrination classes, no further statements were made nor questions answered by the accused. Hence, he did not, over a period of time, hold intercourse with the enemy."

"But he did initially consort with the Chinese officer and did answer questions and thereby did conduct intercourse with the enemy," the JAG sputtered his rejoinder.

"Sir," Goines turned to the law officer. "The wording of Article 104 does not include the verb conduct. The specific and operant words are hold intercourse. As the JAG has just emphasized, the accused did not hold intercourse over a prolonged period of time."

"And your reference for such a limiting use of words?" The law officer asked.

"The defense offers *Webster's Third International Dictionary* as exhibit. The first four definitions in the referenced dictionary specify that hold refers to over a prolonged period of time. The clear statement is that two different and separate occasions do not constitute a prolonged period of time."

Goines handed the references to the law officer and returned to his table, but he was not through presenting evidence.

"I add, Sir, General Order 54-3, Headquarters, Fourth Army, dated 1 January 1954. It states that in all military correspondence and formal proceedings within this command, the dictionary just referenced is to be the official source of definitions."

Goines then handed a copy of the specified General Order to the Law Officer.

In the stifling silence, Goines returned to his table and stood as at attention, eyes fixed on a point some six inches above the head of the Presiding Officer. In the silence interrupted only by whispers among the press representatives, the law officer reviewed first one item of evidence then the other. After a thorough study by the law officer, the decision.

Major Smathers cleared his throat. "In view of the exhibits submitted and the statements as to the limited number of instances in which the accused did meet with the Chinese, the motion for dismissal by the defense is sustained. All charges based on the specifications under Article 104, are dismissed."

A buzz grew as the evidence was handed to the President of

the Board. Colonel Simpson smiled, almost, at Captain Goines' good work. Goines took this opportunity to lean over to Cronwette and whisper, "At least they can't hang you."

A repeat of the process regarding Article 105 had no surprise. No bombshell.

"In support of the charge of violation of Article 105, to wit, misconduct as a prisoner, the evidence is that the accused, Corporal Bertram J. Cronwett did, secure favor in the form of extra food, for violation of the known code of conduct that the prisoner shall give only name, rank, and serial number to the enemy."

True to the warning from Captain Goines the trial did proceed focused on Article 105 in a tedious and boring fashion.

"Article 105 specifies conduct in time of war. Congress did not declare war." Captain Goines protested.

"Presidential Order specified that all activities relative to the Korean Police Action shall be considered as in time of war," rebutted JAG.

"One piece of fish at one meal in a small cup of gruel can't be considered favorable treatment," Goines countered.

"The UCMJ does not indicate limits on size or amount of any favorable treatment, only that some form, regardless of size, of special treatment be given," the lieutenant rejoined.

To the relief of the law officer, the evidentiary phase of the trial was completed and summary statements given before Colonel Simpson's limit of 1200 hours. The members of the court retired to the stuffy ante-room for deliberations. In the small unfurnished room the members each availed themselves of a cup of coffee and a roll. They stood awkwardly juggling the items as they waited in the unusually warm airlessness for the colonel to initiate deliberations.

"Sir, is a question in order at this time?" Major Oswald J. Montoya waited.

Colonel Simpson, as both designated presiding member of the Board and ranking officer, was determined to move the proceedings as quickly possible. Even though necessary to meet the stipulations of the UCMJ regarding time for deliberations Colonel Simpson was punctilios in crossing all needed letters of deliberation and covering any and all questions of content, smartly. "Yes, Major Montoya, please open our discussion." Colonel Simpson smiled.

"We have no question that the letter of the law contained in Article 105 was violated." Major Montoya began. "Its spirit is questioned is it not, that the accused was trying to learn to read?"

"Is that suggesting that a desire to further one's education is justification for treasonous acts, Major?" Colonel Simpson kept his face bland.

"Well, Sir, it's not a question of treason, per se. My concern was for a clarification of the accused's intent and its possible impact on the deliberations," the major explained.

"Bear in mind, gentlemen, that this Article does not include any reference to intent." Colonel Simpson addressed himself to all the members. "If the act, not subject to the considerations of intent or other circumstances, is committed, we have guilt."

"And we have no question but that he did speak beyond the stipulated name, rank, and serial number," Captain Roland L. Smith, West Point class of '41, added. He wanted to be part of the discussion yet wanted to be careful about it. A realist, Smith, like Captain Goines, knew that fullbird colonels had a way of becoming generals. Generals had specific ways to tend to promotions of aspiring captains in either positive or negative ways.

"Captain, we set limits on information that may be given the enemy by prisoners. Cronwette did stand in indoctrination class and make statements construed as in support of a foreign ideology. His statements offered no real aid to an enemy as would divulging plans or order of battle. Does it not seem merely a case of misconduct?" Major Montoya pressed.

"Then to the charge, you say, guilty?" Smith responded.

"Not really," Montoya clarified. "I'm asking the extent that prior suggestions even veiled as brainwashing, may have impacted on Cronwette during what he thought were reading lessons."

"Brainwashing and not to his knowledge?" Smith asked.

"One may have observed that the accused doesn't appear of sufficient intelligence to know the actual content of any material to which his so called reading lessons exposed him," Montoya persisted.

"Are you suggesting brainwashing as a defense?" Colonel Simpson broke in.

"Not so much a defense, Sir." Montoya responded. "I do however suggest it is a circumstance which the accused would not have realized was taking place, if it did take place."

"Then," Colonel Simpson smiled, "you suggest that the circumstance is an unknown."

"Well, yes, Sir." Montoya knew he was checked.

"Major, gentlemen, the Department of the Army has specifically ordered that a question of brainwashing is not, in and of itself, an excuse for or mitigation to any officer or enlisted, while a prisoner of war, to provide information beyond name, rank, and serial number."

Colonel Simpson paused to give his words a moment to sink in. "One thing I hear all of you saying is that you have no question as to whether or not the statements were made. Since we are in agreement the accused is in violation of Article 105, I suggest we vote." He finished and turned to the law officer. "Major, please?"

The law officer handed each member of the Board a small prepared slip of paper. On one end of the paper was printed the word 'GUILTY' and the words 'NOT GUILTY' on the opposite end. He instructed them, "Tear the slip of paper in two. Give the half representing your vote, back to me for counting. As the release of Lieutenant Bartles reduces the number of members to an even number, in case of a tie, I am required to cast the deciding vote."

The room was silent except for the tearing of paper. The law officer collected the votes as presented, counted them and gave them to Colonel Simpson for count verification. Once Colonel Simpson nodded that he had completed his count, the law officer cleared his throat and announced the findings.

"The accused is found guilty of violation of Article 105 of the Uniform Code of Military Justice. Your task is now to assess punishment."

"What are the punishment options?" Major Montoya had been rebuffed, but was not withdrawing from what he saw as fast becoming a one-sided process.

"The Code specifies for violation of this article," Major Smathers glanced at the manual for a second. "Such punishment as the court in deliberation may assess."

"Then we may assess any sentence from simple company-punishment to death?"

"No," the law officer pointed to the manual. "Death is not an option under this article. The most severe sentence may be a combination of dishonorable discharge, forfeiture of all pay and allowances, loss of all awards and citations, and life at hard labor. Not death."

"My God! What's the difference?" Captain Smith blurted.

"Captain, we're here to serve the requirements of the Code, not to editorialize," Colonel Simpson corrected.

"Excuse me, Colonel, I was struck by an obvious equating of the two as terminals of similarity." Captain Smith struggled mentally to find an adequate cover for his outburst, then decided to leave it alone. "Just a thought, Sir."

"As I look at the issue, it seems to be a pure lack of perspective on the part of the accused." Major Montoya would not allow his concept of justice to be ground under the wheels of military rank's obvious push to judgment. "We should consider his feeling that he lacked freedom of choice in the camp."

Master Sergeant Herman L. Fenton, enlisted representative on the Board interrupted. "Sir, with due respect to the Major, he had the same choice as others who did not speak in the indoctrination. Did he not?"

"We deal, Sergeant Fenton, with the question from his perspective. There were instances that may have vitiated his idea of freedom of choice. First, was the beating of Sergeant Pate. Second was the possibility of an easier rapport that captive and captor established in the individual sessions with the Chinese officer who convinced Cronwette it was a reading lesson."

To prevent a rebuttal from Colonel Simpson, Montoya did not pause. "Had the captors shown by their behavior and subterfuges, at least in Cronwette's mind that there was no freedom of choice?"

"Just a minute on the question of the beating of Sergeant Pate." Colonel Simpson stepped back into the discussion. "The operators of the camp were military. Our enemy but a military organization. Not one of you would accept such abusive language, not even you, Sergeant Fenton, in a military formation. We'd chose other forms of punishment, to be sure, but we'd certainly effect some form of discipline."

Silence was achieved. For an awkward minute the five men stood nervously sweating. Finally Major Montoya opened his line of thought.

"One point I'd like to consider, Sir. We have not only the statements from other POWs but the accused's own statement that he did speak more than the limited name, rank, and serial number, a violation of Article 105. But on that point of speaking, alone, we must charge others not included in this charge or specifications. It's unrealistic to even imagine any captured soldier saying nothing to any captor in any POW camp, beyond name, rank, and serial number."

"We have no testimony on that point," Colonel Simpson said.

"Sergeant Pate, for example, Sir." Major Montoya spoke softly.

"He was the ranking enlisted. It was his responsibility to maintain military order and discipline among all enlisted US troops, Major." Captain Smith spoke for Colonel Simpson hoping possibly to cover his earlier outburst. "He was therefore duty bound to function in that capacity."

"But, Captain, you make my point." Major Montoya smiled. "Intent. Sergeant Pate's intent you noted. The accused's intent was to recount learned information as proof of his new skill. His intent was not to give aid and comfort to the enemy. If we excuse Sergeant Pate's action because of a presumption of intent, should we not allow the same for the accused?"

"Colonel Battencourt," Colonel Simpson broke into the discussion in an effort possibly to draw the conversation away from Montoya. "If I remember correctly, you were in Korea in 1950. You've been quiet in this discussion. Please give us your assessment of the accused's conduct. Would you say he was an example of the qualities of the men with whom you had contact?"

"Well, I don't consider myself any judge, especially since I'm not a line officer. I was there, only briefly," Battencourt reached to adjust his tie. "An inspection for HQ supply, Sir." The lieutenant colonel's face seemed to relax. "What I saw in the tour of supply was a disgrace for the American army, Sir. M-1s with broken stocks, not close to TO & E, some men without combat boots."

"Excuse me, Colonel, we know of the poor equipment, but what of the men you did observe. Was this person an exception when compared to the other men you saw?" Colonel Simpson pressed but unknowingly offered a prompt to Battencourt's desperate mind.

"Well, from my brief experience there," possibly recalling Cronwette's ability to take charge and instill a will to fight into the raw troops, "his behavior was not typical." Battencourt held his breath.

"Thank you, Colonel. Any more questions?" Colonel Simpson looked around the room.

"Sir."

Though facing the opposite end of the room, Colonel Simpson recognized Major Montoya's voice and struggled to keep his face composed as he turned.

"Yes, Major?"

"I'd like to consider some of the statements as being simple efforts by the stronger members of the group to peck." The Major spoke easily.

"That, Sir, requires an explanation." Colonel Simpson's voice betrayed his strain only slightly.

"Certainly, Sir. I grew up on a dirt farm south of here. Mother raised chickens to supplement both income and available foods. Chickens will turn on a sick or weak member of the flock, even from the same hatching. They'll peck the weak ones to death if not stopped," Montoya explained.

"I think the connection is still missing, Major." It was almost spoken as an accusation by Colonel Simpson.

"Following the analogy, Sir, we know that POWs become easily paranoid. They are abused and helpless to strike back at the captor. The captor is too strong. There are instances when a POW will attack another but they attack the fellow inmate mostly because they feel abused and paranoid.

Montoya quickly continued, "From Freedom Gate we took them to Inchon, put them on a boat and said that they were back home. We also told them we wanted statements from them about any other POW who caused problems or cheated by turning against them or the American system to get favors. My point, Sir, is that we gave them permission, actually invited them, like a flock of chickens, to peck on the lesser or weaker members of the flock.

"Cronwette was a weak member of the flock. He was seen getting extra favors. They couldn't have turned on the captors in the camp, on the boat we invited them to take out their frustrations on any others. Cronwette became the target for their pecking."

Montoya ended his presentation in a dead silence of thoughtfulness.

"Interesting." Colonel Simpson mused. There was logic in the major's observation. "And their pecking was?" Colonel Simpson looked inquiringly at Major Montoya.

"Making statements became like a snowball rolling downhill, Sir. Each tried to remember the worst that happened. Blame it on Cronwette. Peck on Cronwette. We unknowingly encouraged them to peck by encouraging statements." Montoya was hopeful.

A new trickle of sweat slipped down Colonel Simpson's spine. How to refute that? "It does provide a certain logic, however," a sudden insight into questions of the mind's workings, "we don't have the task of analyzing POW mentality at release." The Colonel visibly relaxed. "We'll leave such psychological analysis to the specialists in the Medical Corps." He waited a moment to let that register then pushed for closure. "We've decided that Cronwette did violate Article 105. He did receive a favor for giving more than name, rank, and serial number. I will not say this to influence any other vote, I must consider the harm done to the Army by the actions of the guilty."

Lieutenant Colonel Battencourt became most intent. He leaned forward a bit to hear Colonel Simpson.

"The press and radio are censuring the Army." Colonel Simpson paused only a moment. "They charge that we are not and have not in the past properly trained our men. Congress is considering hearings on military training and the expenditure of budget. At this point the entire nation's perception of the Army's quality of preparation rests on this one case. Did we not train our soldiers adequately prior to 1950? In view of the threat to the Army in the handling of this case, I will consider the most severe punishment possible as appropriate. A measure must be set in place, a message sent, loud and clear. The Army does not squander its budget, we train our men well, and do not coddle deviation and bad apples."

Simpson finished his summation and glared about the room. The silence was heavy but he did not tarry to drive at his goal. "I propose sentence be set at dishonorable discharge, forfeiture of all pay and allowances, stripping of all awards and citations, and the guilty be confined at hard labor for the rest of his natural life." Silence lay heavy in the room when Colonel Simpson finished his proposed vote. Seizing that as an advantage, he pressed his point.

"I ask for a vote, now. All those in agreement with my call for a life sentence, raise your hand." Colonel Simpson spoke in clear and even tones.

Could a message to the subordinates be read into the colonel's request?

All hands rose, even Montoya's.

"Thank you. We can return to our regular duties. This duty is completed."

As he set down his cup, Major Montoya mumbled an aside to Captain Smith. Nearby Battencourt did not hear the comment. He was most eager to hear all opinions and turned to Montoya.

"A question?"

"A rhetorical one, Sir. I wondered relative to the cliche of spoils going to the victor."

"What do you mean?" Battencourt was confused.

"If the spoils go to the victor, what goes to the victim? But, as I commented, we just gave it to one victim."

CB CB CB

During the long wait in the courtroom, Cronwette had not

answered the question which Captain Goines now repeated.

"Do you know a member of the court?"

"Yes, Sir."

"Which one?" Captain Goines leaned forward.

"That Lieutenant Colonel."

"Battencourt?" Goines pressed.

"Yes, Sir."

"Ever serve under him?"

"Once." Cronwette allowed unenthusiastically.

"Where?"

"Korea."

"On the line?"

"Just once."

Goines looked steadily at the skinny young GI. The chances of this kid getting time in Fort Levenworth was almost certain. What would this information offer in an appeal? How was the relationship that one time in Korea?

"How did you get to know him?"

"Well, it was early. One element of Task Force Smith had just got kicked off a road block. Us survivors took about a week of dodging around rice paddies and among them hills to get back to a friendly unit." Cronwette recited devoid of emotion.

"How early was this?" The Captain dug for details.

"It was real early, you know, Task Force Smith? Hell, they called us a force. Truth was we couldn't force a fart against them NKPA."

"Not enough men or not enough fire power?"

"It don't make no never mind. They's guys there who was wearing tennis shoes cause the Army didn't have boots. That radio they give us was all dirty and too weak to reach headquarters over them damn hills. It was a joke to think we'd stop the T-34s."

"No heavy artillery?"

"Hell, Captain, Sir, the biggest we had was a light and a heavy .30 caliber."

"A road block against tanks with machine guns?" The Captain was astounded. "My first road block was in Germany, late 1944. I was scared as hell and we had two .75 mm. recoilless rifles, two

157

heavy mortars with high explosive anti-tank shells, and a 155 howitzer at each end of our line. How could the Army..."

"Court is now in session."

All rose as the Board filed in behind the table to their seats. Bert kept his eyes on Battencourt. The colonel, however kept his eyes averted. He busied himself with a piece of paper, the table, anything but Bert.

"The law officer will receive the findings of the court." At Colonel Simpson's statement Major Smathers marched front and center, saluted and was given the packet of official papers by Colonel Simpson. The major returned to his seat at the law officer table.

The silence in the hot, muggy room was heavy as the press representatives waited breathlessly for the dash to the phone.

Colonel Simpson cleared his throat and looked at the accused. "It is the finding of this court that Corporal Bertram J. Cronwette is guilty of violation of Article 105, Uniform Code of Military Justice, as specified in the charge. The guilty will present himself to the Court for sentencing."

At Captain Goines' direction, Bert stepped from behind the defense table, marched as best he could still working with his lingering limp, to a spot approximately two feet from the court's table, and saluted.

Colonel Simpson did not return the salute. He looked hard at Cronwette standing at attention and holding his salute. "The prisoner is reminded that convicted of violation of the UCMJ, he no longer has the privilege of rendering or receiving a military salute."

Bert's hand wavered then dropped to his side. A deep flush swept over the crestfallen youth's drawn face.

Colonel Simpson continued. "You, Bertram John Cronwette have been found guilty of violation of Article 105 of the Uniform Code of Military Justice in that you did give aid and comfort to the enemy while a prisoner of war in Manchuria."

Colonel Simpson paused looked sternly at Bert for a minute before he asked. "Do you wish to make a statement before sentence is pronounced?"

"Well, ah Sir..." Bert started a bit hesitantly, took a breath, gained enough composure, and continued. "I's as good a soldier as I knowed. I'll still do the best I can. If it's alright, Sir, they's another thing I'd like to say."

Colonel Simpson did not change his steely glare so Bert continued.

"They's one officer a sittin' on your Board and wearing a Combat Infantry Badge. That badge, they told me when they give me mine, is for enlisted men and junior officers who stand against an armed enemy."

"This here'n," Bert unceremoniously ripped his badge from his shirt and laid it almost reverently on the table in front of the surprised Colonel. "I give this to him to wear. Mine's different from the one he's a wearin'" Bert paused and in as steady and direct a voice as his emotions would allow him to muster, finished, "'cause this'n was earned."

Colonel Simpson, surprised but task focused said, "The sentence of this court is that you, Bertram John Cronwette be dishonorably discharged from the Army, stripped of all awards, citation, and commendations, forfeit all pay and allowances, and be confined at hard labor for the remainder of your natural life."

Chapter 12

Aftermath

"General Prisoner Cronwette!"

Bert jumped. Warned about tardiness by the guard yesterday, Bert scurried to the cell door. He made it in time, standing at attention when the guard stopped at the cell door.

"Visitor." The big MP Guard growled as he unlocked the door. He swung the cell door open, moved to one side and grumbled, "Four steps forward, march."

Bert complied.

"Right face, forward march." The command was low and guttural. At the door leading from that cell wing of the Fourth Army Stockade, the guard muttered, "Halt."

Bert remained at attention as the guard spoke through the barred door to a second guard, "Pass General Prisoner Cronwette to interrogation."

The door was unlocked, opened, and the command given to march. Bert complied carefully and quickly to avoid more stabs in the kidney by a guard's baton. He still winced at times from the first day's mistakes.

Marched into the small interrogation room, Bert was surprised to see Roy Hudson, his friend from the troop ship. Hudson was in uniform and wore sergeant's stripes. The contrast to Bert's garb of denim fatigues, low quarters, no shoe laces, and no belt was substantial.

"Hello, Bert." Roy turned to the guard. "Thank you, this interview will concern classified information and is considered confidential. I have gained permission previously for a confidential interrogation. You may check with the Desk Sergeant."

The guard looked closely at Hudson, "You have been informed about not giving any items to the prisoner?"

"Yes I have, and agreed to comply, thank you."

The guard left after giving Bert a sour look. The guard closed the door and locked it. The guard hurried down the corridor to the Desk Sergeant's office. "Sarge that visitor for Cronwette said I couldn't stay in the room."

The sergeant didn't look up from the magazine he was reading. "PMO cleared it 'bout an hour ago. Just wait outside the room."

Meanwhile, Bert had relaxed after shaking Roy's hand and at Roy's gesture, slumped into one of the straight backed chairs by the table. He laid an arm on the table in front of him.

"I won't ask how you're doing, Bert. First, the limp is still no better and I see a bit of a mouse under that one eye."

"They's real anxious to have you sit up at attention when you eat, and make you march everywhere, I found out."

"I'm sorry, Bert. Truly."

"If'n it didn't hurt it'd be funny that they kick you out of the army but make you march, stand, and sit at attention worse than basic training."

"The army doesn't always make sense, Bert."

"Anyhow I thank you fer coming by, Roy."

"Well, it's business, Bert."

"What'cha need?"

"Colonel Simpson went straight to the CG after the trial and got permission to investigate your implication that one of the members of the Board was not entitled to wear the CIB. He got Fourth Army G-2 to task 112th CIC with doing a background check on the other three officers. I suspect it was Battencourt, so I started here with you."

"Oh, I don't reckon it matters that much."

"Well," Roy smiled. "It sure does to Colonel Simpson. He's boiling under his collar, being the..." Roy stopped his sentence, looked carefully around the room for a possible bug, then continued in a milder manner than he had originally spoken, "stickler he is for regulations."

"Oh, he shouldn't be upset 'bout that."

"Don't worry, he couldn't care less for you. In his army a regulation is a regulation and must be followed to the letter. He won't rest until the malcreant is identified and punished for wearing unauthorized decorations and/or ribbons. He wants somebody's ass. Since we had talked on the troop ship, my Operations Officer suggested I might talk with you first, before doing a full-blown investigation."

It was quiet for a minute, so Roy added, "All I need is the name and some details."

Bert dropped his gaze and shrugged again. One limp hand swept across the table top as if clearing it of crumbs.

"Is that an answer, Bert?" Roy prompted.

"It just don't matter no more." Again Bert shrugged.

"All of this has certainly got to be crushing in on you, Bert."

"It's sure more than I figured."

"I can see," Roy pointed to the bruise. "You're getting knocked around and it will continue at Levenworth by both other prisoners and the guards."

"Life is full of rules, ain't it, Roy? And, you know, that's the funny thing 'bout it." Bert was silent for a longer time than Roy expected.

Roy prompted, "Funny thing about what, Bert?"

"Funny 'bout rules." Bert murmured.

Roy waited for Bert this time. "Funny how rules can be different for different folks in the same place told to do the same job."

"Like which different folks, Bert?"

"Like me and that lieutenant colonel, course he's a captain then but we's both told to take that hill and support the two attacks." Bert was still then like a radio play-by-play announcer waiting for another event in the action only he could see. Then the action continued. "When them first shells hit he just went to pieces. He's running and screaming at us that we was to abandon the hill."

The play-by-play ended as Bert looked up with a plaintive sigh. "He done a real Hank Snow, Roy." A moment of silence

162

then, almost as an afterthought, "Poor bastard."

Roy watched Bert's sad face for a minute then asked, "Why do you call him poor? He left you and the rest of the command on that hill to face the enemy."

It was silent for a moment, then Roy saw a wan smile tug at the corners of Bert's mouth and said, "Don't you see, Roy. Rest of my life I'll be just General Prisoner Cronwette who only wants to learn to read. Why every morning I can look in the mirror and see just me, General Prisoner."

Bert was silent. Roy prodded, "And Lieutenant Colonel Battencourt?"

"Oh he'll hafta face a sniveling coward who ran."

Roy sat in silence for a moment and smiled at Bert, "You can open his mirror to the world, Bert. You have the power in one simple statement to let the world see the real Battencourt."

Bert looked back, "Then what?"

"For openers, there's a chance to find the real problem with your reading. One of the faculty at Our Lady of the Lake College, here in San Antonio is doing research with reading disabilities. As an expert witness in a re-trial, she may be able to prove the existence of your problem. Further proof that you were sincere in believing the Chinese were helping with your reading." Roy explained.

"That don't make no difference. That UCMJ book says that the why don't matter."

"Yes, Bert but an appeal is the next step and almost assured under current regs," Roy urged.

"Ain't worth the bother, Roy. They says I's guilty."

"But, Bert," Roy pleaded, "with the decision nullified because of Battencourt, a new Board will have to be appointed. The trial will be held new with a new Board and with the research available, there's a good chance."

"I doubt it, after all the vote was uni-. . . unami-. . . . They all voted the same, guilty. It don't matter about Battencourt cause all the others said I's guilty same as he did."

"An appeal would have to be heard by a new group of officers, Bert, don't you see?"

After a moment of silence Bert looked at Roy. "You don't see, Roy. That recruiter cheated. I couldn't pass that test for enlisting, then or now. I can't change that. Battencourt being exposed to the world can't change that."

As Bert paused, Roy started to speak but Bert raised a hand. "No. Nothing can be changed. I liked the army, the life, being a soldier, but I can't do that no more. If an appeal was in my favor, I still couldn't get back in the army. I just can't change what I want to change."

"And so you say you'll live with it as is?" Roy was puzzled.

"Roy, I never got many choices. I's born skinny, brownish eyes, and can't read. That ain't gonna change. Only met one person who really tried to help me."

"You mean like that sergeant in Japan?" Roy asked.

"Yea, John England was a good man, but," Bert smiled a bit thinly as he continued, "then, 'course his helpin' me meant his job as platoon sergeant would be easier. Even so, 'cept for a few like him, the world's full of me firsters."

"Oh?" Roy pushed.

"The teacher at the Mill school was not a me firster. She worked hard tryin' to help me. I know she tried to help others, too. All she got for her trouble was the skimmed parts."

"What do you mean by skimmed parts, Bert?"

Bert sighed. "She got a room in the mill superintendent's house and three meals a day. Summer time she'd get a bus ticket to visit her folks. That was all she's paid. What she got for her work and helpin' was what's left at the mill after others got to carry off the fat. She got the skimmed parts."

"But, isn't it important that she helped?" Roy asked.

"I say the important part is that helpers usually seem to all get the skimmed parts. You seem like a good 'nuff guy. Don't get no job teachin'."

"But, Bert, many are needed as helpers, doctors, nurses, preachers..."

"Careful on your 'samples, there. I can't recall seein' too many skinny preachers." Bert interrupted. "The best parts of the milk goes to the takers, the helpers in life get the skimmed parts."

In futile thought, Roy sat down-cast for a minute then looked back up, "Your logic is hard to dispute, but what will you do, now?"

"I made up my mind. I gonna do the best as I can with what I got, what I am, and where I am. Roy, strugglin' again your destiny is like shoveling air out'n a hole. It won't make no difference."

Roy sat quietly for a while, then stood and knocked on the door. As the guard unlocked the door Bert jumped to attention.

Roy held out a hand, "You're a better man than I. They'd get a lot of fighting, screaming, cussing, and scraping 'till they threw dirt in my face."

"Life's gonna be, Roy. All a man's fightin' won't change his destiny."

Epilog

An Army Adjutant General spokesperson informed me that as part of the Bicentennial Celebration, 1975, then President Jimmy Carter issued amnesty to those convicted of violation of the Uniform Code of Military Justice while held Prisoner of War by the North Koreans and/or Chinese, 1950 to 1953.

All records of trial, conviction, and incarceration were expunged. For that reason and the fact that the author was proscribed from keeping notes of 1953 interviews with repatriates during Operation Big Switch, this work is a period fiction and not written as nonfiction.

Many dates, locations, military units, and movements may have been altered to fit the story based on memories of those reaptriates interviewed September 1953.

"Bert" is actually a composite of at least two repatriates. Of course I should add, all names and characterizations are fictitious.

Glossary

ADC: Assistant Division Commander. Designee to replace the Division Commander in case of Commander's disability.

AFQT: Armed Forces Qualification Test was used to determine each inductee's mental capacity for training, assignments, and basic potential to military.

Basic Branch: Each officer receives a commission in a branch of the service consistent with his/her initial training. In 1950, this generally included the three arms for army officers, e.g., infantry, armor, artillery. Support branches such as financial, signal corps, chemical corps, etc., were also basic branches.

BAR: Browning Automatic Rifle rapidly fired a .30 caliber round. Light weight, could be fired from the hip with shoulder strap attached, from the prone or sitting positions.

Bazooka: Rocket launcher fired a small explosive projectile. Fired from shoulder or the prone positions. In various sizes, the smallest of which would not penetrate tank armor.

Carbine: Smallest of the .30 caliber weapons used in 1950, was capable of individual or rapid fire.

CG: Commanding General.

CIB: Combat Infantry Badge is awarded to each enlisted man and company-grade officer who serves in action against an armed enemy.

CIC: Counter Intelligence Corps. Army personnel specially trained in interrogation, investigation of personnel and incidents to protect the Army Establishment from treason, sedition, sabotage, and espionage.

Chief of Staff: The officer responsible for coordinating the support staff of a unit commander.

CO: Commanding Officer.

CP: Command Post.

EUSA: Eighth United States Army. (Later EUSAK, the K added for Korea.)

FECOM: Far East Command.

First John: Slang expression referring to a first lieutenant.

Fox Hole: A hole dug in the ground for cover from enemy fire.

Grease Gun: Small machine gun that fired .45 caliber rounds.

G-1: Staff responsible primarily for personnel affairs.

G-2: Staff responsible for intelligence.

G-3: Staff responsible for plans and training.

G-4: Staff responsible for supplies.

GI Party: Complete cleaning of barracks, quarters, latrines, etc. by resident GIs.

Hank Snow: Country singer, well-known and quoted by GIs in Korea. In early fighting the term "bug-out," meaning to run away, was anathema to cadre and proscribed in some units with court martial penalties. Based on a popular ballad by Hank Snow, the term used to mean bug out, was either "get short-coupled and long-gone" or "Pull a Hank Snow."

Han Goul: Americanization of Korean for Korea.

HMG: Heavy machine gun was water cooled, tripod mounted, crew-served, and fired .30 caliber rounds.

How Able: In 1950 military phonetic alphabet was used to refer to "Haul Ass," or   bug out.

KP: Kitchen police was a rotating duty in all military units in the 1950s. The duty assigned to lower rank enlisted men to clean the kitchen area and the mess hall after meals and help, as assigned, with meal preparation.

KIA: Killed in action.

LMG: Light machine gun was air-cooled, tripod mounted, crew-served, and fired the .30 caliber round.

M-1: The basic infantry weapon of the 1950s. Gas-operated, clip-fed, with bayonet attachment it fired .30 caliber rounds.

Mee Goul: Americanization of the Korean term for American.

MLR: Main Line of Resistance was the front line of each army and the point at which enemy attacks were launched.

NCO: Non Commissioned Officer was considered to be the enlisted grades of corporal, in some cases, but always sergeant or above. The cadre.

NCOIC: Non Commissioned Officer In Charge.

NKPA : North Korean Peoples Army.

OIC: Officer In Charge.

Ooutpost: A small group of two or more members of a unit in an advanced location. Its purpose was to give warning to the main unit of any enemy presence.

Pipeline: Enlisted personnel shipped overseas were sent to a collection destination, a Replacement Depot. Individual unit assignments were not available prior to leaving pipeline status at the Replacement Depot, or Repl Depot.

POW: Prisoner of War.

RCT: Rifle Combat Team consisting of varied size units built around a basic rifle company or regiment. Also can refer to a regimental combat team consisting of regimental size unit without minor support personnel.

Rifle Pit: Scooping out dirt to allow the rifle-man quick cover, later may be enlarged.

Road Block: An effort to deny an advancing enemy use of a road by a unit usually with attached armor or artillery.

ROK: Republic of Korea.

ROKA: Republic of Korea Army.

R & R: Rest and recreation leave in a non-combat area. In Korea, after 1950, R&R usually meant Japan. Some opportunities existed for R&R in Hong Kong and Hawaii. The GI was flown to the R&R center, issued Class A uniform, given five days free, then flown back to the basic unit in Korea, minus dress uniform. (It is noted that the dress uniform, was not worn in Korea by enlisted men.)

Second John: Slang expression denoting a second lieutenant.

Show-Down Inspection: An inspection in which each person must display all assigned equipment and clothing. Occasionally used to help locate any missing gear and/or validate unit records.

Slickie-Slickie Boys: Thieves and/or con artists.

SOI: Summary of Investigation.

Spotter: In artillery particularly a spotter or forward observer as close to the enemy as practical and concealed in order to give information on enemy activities for use in directing fire from other concealed location.

TI&E Troop: Troop Information and Education is responsible for dissemination of information and in non-combat, educational opportunities to military personnel.

TO&E: Table of Organization and Equipment is a regulation assigning number, rank, and equipment for each army unit. To not be TO&E is to be lacking in some respect from the regulations.

WIA: Wounded in action.

About the Author

Jerry Carson is a 1946 graduate of high school in Harlingen, Texas and a 1951 graduate of Texas A&I. Drafted into the Army in 1951, he spent August of 1952 through September of 1953 in Korea and returned as part of the de-briefing team taking statements from repatriated POWs during Operation Big Switch.

After military service, Carson entered teaching and at night school earned his Master's and Advanced Certificate in Counseling from University of Maryland. He earned his EdD in Higher Education Administration from NOVA University. His teaching career ended after 36 years with his retirement in 1993.

Jerry and his wife, Mae, live in Georgetown, Texas. The four children and assorted grandchildren and great-grandchildren all live in Maryland. Jerry now spends his time in community work, weaving, and writing.

To order additional copies of
The Guilty of the Korean War

Name _____

Address _____

_____

$16.95 x _____ copies =   _____

Sales Tax   _____
(Texas residents add 8.25% sales tax)

Please add $3.50 postage and handling per book   _____

Total amount due: _____

Please send check or money order for books to:

Jerry Carson
P.O. Box 2117
Georgetown, TX 78627

For a complete catalog of our books, visit our site at
http://www.WordWright.biz

Printed in the United States
3827